Frode Grytten was born in 1960 and grew up in Odda, in the west of Norway. He worked as a reporter for fifteen years and has since published two novels, both widely acclaimed across Europe, and short stories and books for children. He now lives in Bergen.

THE SHADOW IN THE RIVER

One June night, in a town gripped by a heat wave, a man is forced off the road and into the river. Robert Bell, a local journalist, investigates the mysterious death. Meanwhile, simmering racial tensions in the town threaten to boil over, with local Serbian immigrants becoming targets for blame. Robert's brother, Frank, is the investigating police officer, but there's long been a gulf between them, and Robert's in love with Frank's wife Irene. Their affair continues through the stifling heat until one morning Irene vanishes. Is her disappearance somehow linked to the young man's death? Storm clouds gather as Robert is drawn ever deeper into the hunt for a murderer — and finds out some uncomfortable truths about his seemingly quiet community.

FRODE GRYTTEN
Translated by Robert Ferguson

◆

THE SHADOW
IN THE RIVER

Complete and Unabridged

ULVERSCROFT
Leicester

First published in Great Britain in 2007 by
Abacus, an imprint of
Little, Brown Book Group, London

First Large Print Edition
published 2008
by arrangement with
Little, Brown Book Group, London

British Library CIP Data

Grytten, Frode, *1960* –
    The shadow in the river.—Large print ed.—
    Ulverscroft large print series: mystery
    1. Detective and mystery stories
    2. Large type books
    I. Title
    839.8'2374 [F]

    ISBN 978–1–84782–134–8

Published by
F. A. Thorpe (Publishing)
Anstey, Leicestershire

Set by Words & Graphics Ltd.
Anstey, Leicestershire
Printed and bound in Great Britain by
T. J. International Ltd., Padstow, Cornwall

This book is printed on acid-free paper

1

Last night I'd felt a chill in the air, but today would be another hot one. I'd opened all the windows, and a little fan was humming away on the desk. The stink of sweat mingled with the smell of food from the bowling alley in the basement. The odour of hamburgers and chips came wafting up to my office on the fourth floor. I thought I'd read in the paper that the place had gone bust last winter, but now the smell of fast food was spreading through the building.

The phone rang. I just sat there, staring at it. Every five minutes another idiot would call. I sat there calmly until the ringing stopped. A few seconds later the mobile would go. The number displayed was identical to the one on the office phone. A few minutes later some other idiot would go through the same routine. Office phone. Mobile. Office phone again.

I must have taken about twenty calls that morning without getting anywhere. No one wanted to talk, least of all my own brother. I'd rung him around ten. He said nothing. That was odd. Frank once said that everything floats to the surface when a person gets killed. He said it was like pressing a button. People would start talking, even about things they'd kept quiet about for years.

A single piece of paper with notes was all I had. That and a title on the screen: *Summer can't be trusted*. I didn't even know if I'd made it up myself, or if it was something I'd nicked from someone else. That'll have them queuing up at the newsstands, I said to myself: Summer can't be trusted. Had it been an ordinary day they would have asked me to send the stuff over. Send the stuff over, we need a page-filler, they would have said without listening.

I should have taken a shower. My shirt was sticking to my back, and the patches of sweat under my armpits were showing. But the seaplane would soon be dropping down between the mountains. I hated being late, and I hated people who were late. For the last half-hour I'd been playing Solitaire on the computer. *Tripeaks* was a bastard of a game that wouldn't come up. You were only playing for imaginary stakes, but you still got hooked. My standing rule was that I should at the very least break even before I packed it in. Now I got up while I was still down five dollars.

I locked the office door and went

downstairs. The smell in the stairwell made me feel sick and hungry at the same time. I'd gone without breakfast because of all the upset. In the entrance I met three guys. They had to be Serbs or Albanians. I'd seen them here before. Most of the people who went bowling were foreigners. I thought that would suit the owner nicely. A few more consignments of asylum seekers and he'd be able to keep the business going a bit longer, raking in their daily allowance, hiring out bowling shoes, burning a few burgers. Everyone would be happy until the place went bust again in November.

I put my sunglasses on and stepped out into the sunlight. There was too much of it. Someone had gone over the top. My Volvo stood parked over by the church. The coupé stank. The smell had drifted in with the heat. Maybe some leftovers under the seat. Sour milk or something in the boot. I got in. The driver's seat was roasting. It forced me to sit in an uncomfortable position. If anyone saw me they'd laugh themselves sick.

At the junction by the Smeltar Bar I passed my brother. He was driving one of the new Subarus. That was a joke. Police cars should be Volvos. The Volvo had an altogether different authority. When my brother or one of the others came driving along in his

Subaru it looked as if they were playing cops and robbers. Frank didn't see me. He was wearing a short-sleeved uniform shirt and aviator shades, like the ones they wear in American films. I could have reached out and touched him. I was about to shout, whistle, but held back. He turned right and cruised up towards the Co-op Megastore.

It was just after eleven o'clock and the heat had sunk down into the valley. A small cloud had fastened itself to the Folgefonna glacier and looked like a cartoon speech bubble without the writing. I sped past the Hardanger Hotel and the summer wind filled the car. By the Fjord Shopping Centre I braked and indicated right. In the time it took me to drive a few hundred metres to the floating jetty my mobile rang three times.

I walked out on to the jetty with the sensation of falling from a great height. Slowly the tiny dot between the sides of the mountains grew larger and larger. I could see the wings and the propellers. Soon it would hit the surface of the water. On the quay behind people stopped to watch the landing. Even the fat boy on the floating jetty took a break from his stone-throwing. He sat there with a pile of ammunition and watched the seagulls disappearing in the direction of McDonald's.

4

Can you keep watch at night? the boy asked without looking up.

He asked the question as though he already knew the answer. As though he'd asked everyone in Odda, and was now inviting further rejection. The boy spoke good Norwegian. I thought I'd seen him before. He was wearing a Brazil shirt with the name RONALDO on the back.

I have to sleep at night, said the boy. Someone has to keep watch. Or it won't work. I'm not allowed out at night.

I said I wasn't allowed out at night either.

The boy didn't smile. He had a face without a smile.

They took another one last night, he said. Now there's only five left.

How many were there before?

Seven or eight.

I turned towards the bay where a mother duck was swimming about and trying to marshal her ducklings up on to the beach. I counted five. On one of the rocks down there someone had daubed in red paint: *Do not eat the ducks. You will be reported to the police.*

Can you keep watch at night? asked the boy. I was out last night, but I got told off.

I need sleep too, you know.

It's summer, said the boy.

The seaplane hummed towards us. Martinsen climbed out on the right-hand side and got ready to jump ashore. I could almost have believed the guy had flown the plane himself from Bergen to Odda. He was the type to do something like that. He had a pilot's licence and was good at talking people round.

How old are you, Ronaldo? I asked.

Nearly nine, he answered.

A good age, I said.

At last the boy looked up.

Can you keep watch at night? he asked again.

It's summer, I said.

Martinsen stepped ashore with a bag over each shoulder. He wore sunglasses and a white shirt and khaki shorts. I shook his hand and thought of asking him about the trip, or maybe about his pictures from Gaza. One of them had been used the weekend before. Martinsen had even written the piece himself, about how he'd been hit by plastic bullets fired by Israeli soldiers. I hated it when photographers insisted on doing their own writing.

You've got to ring the desk editor, Martinsen said, fiddling with his mobile. She's sent me three messages telling you to ring her.

I tossed his bags into the back of the Volvo

6

and asked if he wanted me to drive to the hotel. Martinsen said he'd prefer to get his bearings first. I thought, well that needn't take long. Just breathe in, turn 360 degrees and breathe out.

Do we have a body? asked Martinsen.

Not to my knowledge, I answered. They're looking over at the river.

Drive me there.

I wound down the window and started the car. In the bay some old man appeared with a bag of breadcrumbs for the ducks. Over by McDonald's the seagulls took off and skimmed across the surface of the water. As I swung out of the parking slot I saw Ronaldo stand up on the jetty and reach out for a stone.

2

The path followed the perimeter of the factory fence. The Opo flowed more quietly here. The frenzy of the rapids higher up was replaced by a sort of resignation. Freshwater met saltwater, and with a kind of a shrug the river abandoned itself to the fjord.

In one of the houses on the other side a woman was cleaning windows. At last there was some point in cleaning windows in Odda. The factory had gone bankrupt at the end of April, and the carbide dust no longer lay like a grey veil over the town. The cranes on the quayside stood motionless. The aerial ropeway had stopped running and the carriages hung in a line from the quay up to Nyland, like full stops in the air. It was as if someone had come creeping up to Odda, put his fingers to his lips, and whispered: *Shhhh!*

The police cordon meant that we got no closer than a hundred metres. People were searching on both sides of the river. Rubber dinghies were crossing back and forth. In the white sunlight it almost looked as though they were out fishing. It was a nice day out on the fjord, and they wanted to see what the fishing was like.

The bloke'll turn up, right? asked Martinsen. A body always floats to the surface, isn't that right?

I didn't know. I'd heard of a man who fell into the river and got dragged off by the undercurrent all the way to Måge, ten kilometres further down the fjord. Another guy wasn't found until months later. By then there was nothing left of him but a skeleton.

Martinsen was taking photographs from the path but said he wanted to try from another angle. He slung a camera over his shoulder and climbed out on to the decaying bridge. The gate was covered in rusty barbed wire. A sign hung on it: *Danger: High Voltage*. It was hard to see what could be dangerous there. The real danger was that the bridge might collapse and you would fall into the river. It could happen to anybody, at any time. The ground could disappear beneath your feet, the sky fall on your head.

I followed Martinsen over the gate and on the way down dropped my sunglasses and cut my left hand on the barbed wire as I tried to catch them. I stood there, staring at my hand. There was no blood at all at first, even though the cut must have been pretty deep. And then out it poured. Typical. Martinsen had hopped elegantly over the top while I, naturally, had to cut my hand.

Martinsen helped me try to staunch the flow of blood with a handkerchief. He took his mobile from his shirt pocket, answered, smiled: Here, you can speak to the man himself. I took the phone with my right hand. Blood was still pumping from my left. It was the desk editor. They always get hold of you, I thought. You can hide and you can run, but in the end they always catch up with you.

Is it a murder? she asked.

Well, at any rate it's bleeding, I said.

I'm sorry?

I sighed.

No body so far, I said. Just a lot of blood.

Blood? Do the police think it's an accident or murder?

They're searching, we're waiting.

I've been trying to get hold of you for the last two hours.

I didn't answer. I pictured her sitting there at head office in Bergen, smiling in some smart suit or other. At the party for the opening of the new building the architect had said something about the glass façade, how it gave outsiders a round-the-clock view of the frenetic activity within. I had stood there with a glass of champagne in my hand, smiling to myself. Almost nothing ever happens in newspaper offices. Editors, desk editors, journalists, all sitting in front of their computer screens. Now and then they stare down into the street, at the people passing by, watch lovers kissing, see drunkards pissing on the glass façade.

Are you there? asked the desk editor.

I'm here, I replied. Where else would I be?

Why don't you answer your mobile?

I've had things to do.

Like what, for example?

Like finding out how all this hangs together.

She ended the conversation: Then do it. We're all trying to pull together here, right?

The bridge was the ideal place from which to follow the search. We should have been closer, but the view wouldn't have been any better. The river flowed swollen and thick with rubbish. It occurred to me that I hadn't been down here since I was a boy. I always thought salmon fishermen used the shelter on the banks, but there was no sign of them. The path beside the river was almost overgrown. It was one of the nicest parts of the whole of Odda, but the factory had obscured it for years. On the west side were the containers and the enormous ventilation pipe known as the steel snake. On the east side were the cranes and the offloading quay. On both sides

11

there was a high fence with barbed wire. The river had been turned into a secret, the river had to be hidden. As though its beauty mustn't be allowed to intrude upon the picture of an ugly, dirty Odda.

I went back along the path. The Pedersen kid had probably floated past here some time in the night. Maybe he'd been carried downstream and under the bridge with the danger sign on it. Maybe he was dead even before he wound up in the Opo. Maybe he'd been pounded to death on the rocks at the bottom of the river. In my mind's eye I saw a white body being carried through dark water. Everything caught it. Everything snagged it. The melt water of the glacier caressing the body one last time.

3

The smell of a sweaty town. The stink of my Volvo. It was funny. Now that Odda had finally got rid of the pollution from the factory, here was I driving round in a car that had such a terrible stench. I wound down the window and turned along the road by the Shell station. The warm steering wheel was sticky with blood.

In the centre of town people strolled about as though it was a normal day. Tourists in cars rolled through the streets, on their way to or from the ferry, gazing through their windscreens at the sleepy town. But there was something different about the town today. Rumours clung to the rooftops and the walls. Gossip spattered, chatter was spread around. Soon all the words would enter and fill the rooms of this town.

Martinsen asked where we could hire a helicopter.

I told him the only place you could get one was from a firm based over in Kinsarvik and Rosendal. It was owned by Samson Nilsen, a retired speedway star who'd moved back home to Odda and gone into tourism. Nilsen had bought up several local firms, including the helicopter company.

I parked outside the Hardanger Hotel while Martinsen rang the desk editor to find out if it was okay about the helicopter. Martinsen said he had good pictures from down by the river but that the readers ought to be given a feeling of the distance involved and the geography.

Six months earlier I'd written something about the investment in helicopter tourism. Samson Nilsen wanted to fly rich people to the glacier at Folgefonna and serve them strawberries and smoked salmon up there. He wanted to build a funicular and create a mountain resort where visitors could come all year round for the slalom skiing, the telemark skiing and snowboarding. He had the support of the locals but central government turned him down. Odda was a Labour Party stronghold that wanted to go into tourism in a big way, but a Conservative minister called a halt to it all, on environmental grounds. I was the first to write about it all; others had taken it up after me.

Martinsen asked if I knew anything about the tabloids.

I hadn't seen anyone apart from journalists from the local papers and I replied that I thought we had a few hours' head start. The desk editor decided in the end that we should just go ahead while they checked the prices from Bergen. Martinsen asked for the name of the helicopter firm.

Viking Air, I answered.

You're joking.

I never joke.

Try Viking Air in Kinsarvik, Martinsen said into his mobile.

I drove up Kremarvegen, passed the Co-op Megastore, the courthouse and the town hall. Then on through Nyland, past the swimming pool and the abandoned factory. My hand was beginning to throb and as we drove I stuck it out of the window as though that would heal it quicker.

I indicated left and cruised across Hjøllo bridge. A group of onlookers had gathered by the railings. I parked halfway across the bridge. Martinsen grabbed his camera and got out. The Opel was still balanced up on its side in the water, like a piece of modern sculpture. Earlier in the day I had thought the current would dislodge the car and carry it away downstream, but somehow the front of it must have got wedged between rocks. The Opel couldn't have been under more than a metre and a half of water. The rest of the chassis was visible. The upper door was half-open, and a couple of the side windows were broken. It looked as if the car had frozen in the last frame of a film. Staring at the wreck you could see all the scenes leading up to it. The Opel coming too fast down the hill. The driver losing control. The car hitting the parapet before pitching over into the river.

The water was the colour of lead. The rushing mass of glacial water made a high, droning sound, like a motor. On the eastern bank was a used-car lot with the cars glinting in the sunlight. When I was a child we started a petition against it. The council had given the owner the precise spot where we used to play football. Every evening we'd play there, and every evening we would have to go after the ball when it ended up in the river. Usually it would bob back to the bank. If not, we had to nick the boat from the foundry and row out into the fjord.

Martinsen returned. He said nothing. I wondered whether to tell him that I had grown up here. There was the football pitch. There was our ski jump. There were the slag heaps. From the bridge you could even see part of our old house. It was on the heights above the river, hidden behind the trees.

What actually happened? asked Martinsen.

I shrugged. There were no witnesses, even though the Opel had ended up in the river right next to the Kingdom Hall. The place

16

had been erected by a crowd of Jehovah's Witnesses in a matter of days. But no one had been there last night.

Is it murder? asked Martinsen.

I didn't know. No one knew. Everything was just rumour. One missing. Two suspects.

Do you know anything about the lad?

I said his name was Guttorm Pedersen. He was nineteen, unemployed, son of the man who drives the ice-cream van.

We drove on up the valley, following the road as it wound along parallel to the river. I held my hand out of the car window. The sun burnt the skin, but the wind cooled it down again. Near the hospital we got stuck behind a German mobile home. Oncoming traffic made it impossible to overtake. The German had a little sticker on the back of his van: *Ich liebe Deutschland*. I wondered why, in that case, he hadn't just stayed at home.

At Sandvin lake I pulled over. The mobile home drove on, heading south. The German had already picked up a pretty good tail behind him. Most of them looked like tourists passing through. A hundred years ago they came to Odda from all over Europe. Now they just drove straight through.

I thought I should maybe take another look at helicopter tourism. If anything new had happened there I might be able to get a story

17

out of it. Anyway, Samson Nilsen had a point. The Fonna glacier and the waterfalls had attracted tourists here right up until the industrial revolution did for Nationalistic Romanticism. Why shouldn't they have another go at attracting tourists now that the factories were on the way out? Nature was a gold mine. The first foreigners came here in the nineteenth century. Englishmen took blocks of blue ice from the glacier back home to London with them. In the gentlemen's clubs it was the smart thing to drink your whisky with exclusive Hardanger ice. *National Geographic* had just voted Hardanger the best tourist destination in the world. But that hardly included the town of Odda.

Martinsen crossed the road and took a couple of general shots of the asylum seekers' hostel. It was a yellow stone building, in a nice spot just where lake became river and Odda became town. The place had been an old people's home when I was growing up. My grandmother spent the last years of her life there. I remember visiting her there one Christmas weekend. She thought I was her son. Then, a couple of years ago, local politicians worked out that old people equalled Expenditure and asylum seekers Income.

I lit a cigarette and inhaled deeply. I felt

better. I was on the move. Something was happening. It was no longer just me and a bunch of idiots who didn't say anything. Martinsen came back and said he wanted to go into the hostel, but that would have to wait until later.

Do you know who the suspects are? he asked.

I shook my head. I'd heard rumours. People said they were Somalis. People thought they were Kosovan Albanians. The Pedersen kid was supposed to have got into an argument with a group of asylum seekers outside Hamburger Heaven the same evening he ended up in the river. There were rumours that the asylum seekers waited for the lad and drove off after him in his Opel.

Martinsen asked me to cruise round a bit. He wanted to see if there was anything he'd missed with his camera. We drove over Eidesmoen, down Tjodalen, past Sing Sing, through Bygda. We crawled along past the police station, the Murboligen estate and the primary school. I indicated and turned out on to the main road.

On Eitrheimsvegen I had to brake hard. An old lady with a walker came swaying out into the road. She was wearing a flowery summer dress and a wig that was in danger of falling off. Traffic came to a halt as the lady tried in slow motion to catch up with her walker.

I nodded to the lady.

Welcome to Odda, I said.

We sat and stared through the windscreen. People milled around in the square. They seemed not to have a plan. I thought, well, that's the way it is in small towns. Things seem unplanned. You have to be a local to know the plan. I knew this place inside out. Everything about it. All the same, Odda was strange viewed through the windscreen. The streets splayed out in white light made the place unrecognisable. And I thought, well, now it looks as if I don't know what the plan is either.

4

The Smeltar was full even though it was the middle of the day. The proprietor had covered the windows with posters and black tape to keep out summer. But there was nothing he could do about the match. There was too much at stake. Too much money involved.

I was supporting Argentina. I'd always liked Argentina. At least when they tried to play football. Now they weren't even trying. Players just passed the ball to the man nearest them. I saw bodies that moved almost without making any progress, as though they were underwater. I recognized the feeling from the days I used to play myself.

The sweat was pouring off me, as though my body had discovered a secret source and was pumping it out at high speed. I was dying for a shower. At regular intervals I felt the mobile vibrating. I didn't answer. I just wanted to stand there in the gloom with the others and watch this lousy football match.

Anything new on the murder? the guy beside me asked.

You tell me.

The guy looked offended.

I am asking you.

I don't know any more than anybody else, I said.

Everybody knows who did it.

He finished his beer and put the glass down.

I asked how he knew it was murder.

I don't know how, he said.

But you asked if there was anything new on the murder?

Murder's murder. Everybody knows that.

So how do you know it was a murder?

What else would it be? D'you think the Petersen kid felt hot and decided to take a dip?

I don't know. I'm not working.

I thought journalists were always working.

I didn't know the man, but he obviously knew me. That was one of the drawbacks of being a journalist working in a small town. Everybody knew who you were. Everybody knew what you did. Everybody thought they could say whatever they liked to you.

Explain one thing to me, said the man. When everybody knows who did a murder, why don't the police just go ahead and arrest them?

I said I didn't know.

Look, he said. Everybody knows who they are, and they can count themselves lucky they never killed a girl.

I said I'd love to know who we were talking about, and exactly why they should count themselves lucky.

Everybody knows those Serbs, said the man. Nothing but trouble. Last night they had a go at the Pedersen kid outside Hamburger Heaven. The police had to pull them apart. If it had been a girl, none of us would have been standing here now. We would've been out there. You get my drift? Out there.

He went off to buy another beer.

I couldn't explain it, but this was a different pub. Maybe it was the match, maybe it was something else, I wasn't sure. I'd been going to the Smeltar every day that week to watch the football. Suddenly there was an air of crudeness about the place. The noisiest fans sat there in their England shirts, shouting at the screen: *Get a haircut, you dago! Get up, you big girl!*

Half an hour into the match England were awarded a penalty. Everyone could see Michael Owen dived but the ref gave the penalty. David Beckham took the kick. A short run-up and the ball was in the back of the net. Argentina went under for the third time. I pushed my way through the cheering throng.

The car stood outside the church. Inside it was baking hot. I pulled out and felt the throbbing in my left hand. I'd shower, change the bandage and get down to some proper work. It was a long time since I'd had a big story. Last time must have been when I wrote about the blind cod that went into the same fish trap over and over again. I got two front pages out of that story, the first when I did a portrait of the cod, and the second when he ate himself to death in the aquarium in Bergen.

Back home at Tokheim the air was musty and close so I opened the veranda door. While I undressed I listened to my messages on the answering machine. Sometimes I deleted them without even listening. I couldn't face the disappointment of yet another day without hearing from Irene. I always regretted it afterwards. Perhaps that had been the very day when she *had* rung.

The first messages were from the paper. One from early in the morning asking me to get in touch, Martinsen from the taxi on his way out to the seaplane, the voices of various bosses. I could draw you a plan of the whole organisation from those messages alone. Normally I didn't hear a thing from them. This was my big day, no doubt about it.

I was standing there with my shirt half over

my head when I heard a familiar voice: Robert, can you meet me tonight? Usual place, ten o'clock?

The voice made me uneasy. I played the message again; maybe there was a subtext, something I'd missed. I walked over to the window and looked down at the zinc factory. A cargo boat was berthed at the quay. The golfers on the course by the bay were no more than moving dots. A seaplane glided down towards the fjord. That would be the tabloids arriving. I thought, well, now we're not alone any more.

I wanted to ring Irene and ask why she wanted to meet me. What had happened? I didn't do it; I had promised that I would never ring. I tried to imagine her. Her face disappeared. I'd thought too much about her. I'd thought her to death.

The phone rang and I picked it up immediately. I hoped it was Irene. I wanted to hear her voice. I wanted to speak to her. She could yell at me, call me the biggest idiot in creation, or tell me to go to hell. I just wanted to hear her voice.

It was Martinsen. He was down by the mouth of the river. They'd found the boy.

5

Two helicopters hovered above the fjord. The thrust from the rotating blades whipped up the water. The sound hit me in the chest and travelled through my body. The disturbance spread to the landscape, as though the sound was changing the place, breaking it down in a slow process of disintegration.

A number of journalists were lined up by the police cordon. I didn't recognise any of them and I couldn't even see Martinsen. Onlookers were standing on the old works bridge. I climbed over to them. Down by the fjord the search parties were gathered at the offloading quay. I caught sight of my brother. Frank gesticulated while he spoke on the mobile. A rubber dinghy approached and a policewoman caught the rope and moored it. A black bag was lifted on to the quay and carried over to a waiting ambulance. Everything happened very efficiently and quickly, as though they'd done it all a hundred times before.

I made a note of the time: a quarter past four. I rang my brother. He didn't answer. Martinsen didn't answer either. One of the helicopters took off and disappeared south-wards. The other remained hovering over the river and then came down even lower. I could see the logo in white on a red background: *Viking Air*.

I stayed where I was until Martinsen called back, his voice almost drowned by the roar. I gathered that *VG* had hired both helicopters. Martinsen had asked the desk at Bergen to check if there were any other helicopters available, but *VG* had secured reserve bookings with all the competing companies too. Martinsen told me that he was waving to me. I looked round and saw him on the containers inside the factory area. I wondered how he'd managed to get up there. There were holes in the fencing — the workers used to use them for sneaking off work or smuggling whisky from the boats.

Then the second helicopter disappeared as well. Suddenly everything went quiet. The only sounds came from the river. I called my brother again. He didn't answer. The man next to me said he knew what I should write.

Oh yeah? What should I write then?

They've got to get rid of the asylum seekers' hostel. Write that. They should get rid of that fucking hostel.

Bad as that?

Write that foreigners are best off in Oslo.

People there are used to weirdness. Here they stand out too much. No. Suppose the farmers along the fjord here started growing olives? Write that.

I asked what that had to do with anything.

The man next to him joined in: The Muslims are taking over. Not now, not next year, but they'll take over all right. It's always the ones who breed most who take over. The Muslims have children all the time, but we're dying out.

I didn't say anything. The desk editor called and I let the phone ring. The first man leaned over towards me. I could smell the sweat on him.

Take this river. Emissions and salmon farming have killed off almost all the wild salmon. Know what I mean?

Not completely.

The Muslims are like salmon from the fish farms. We feed them up, right? We make them strong. One day they swim upriver and take over.

And you're quite sure about this? I asked.

Both helicopters returned, and the man had to shout in my ear to be heard above the roar: Write that we wish the Muslims a pleasant journey home!

I took off my sunglasses and looked at him. Then I clambered over the fence and walked back up along the river bank. Martinsen stood waiting for me by one of the fishing huts. He held his mobile out to me: You're a popular man, he said.

I took the telephone.

There you are, said the desk editor.

Yes, *here* I am, I said.

Martinsen says they've found the boy, she said.

Well, they've found something all right, I said.

What d'you mean?

Someone put something or other into a body bag and someone else put something or other into an ambulance.

The boy?

It could have been a dolphin.

There was silence from the other end. Then a laugh. So she had a sense of humour.

Are there dolphins in South Fjord? she asked.

Yes. They come at the weekends to show off their tricks. The mayor wants to use them. 'Come to Odda — Hardanger's very own dolphin country.'

I thought the fjord was dead because of the emissions?

No, it's packed with dolphins.

There was another pause.

Can you get a picture of the boy?

With a dolphin?

She didn't laugh this time. The joking was over.

We need a picture of the boy, she said. This is going to be a big story.

I gave the mobile back to Martinsen.

We went back up the path, got into the car and drove into the centre of town. Martinsen went to the hotel to send his pictures. I popped into the diner at the Hardanger for a beer and something to eat. It was a quiet afternoon. Tor sat with me at the table while I ate. Tor and I had gone to school together. He'd got the job at the bar when they started cutting back on the workforce at the factory. Tor was no more a cook than I was. The chips weren't hot and the burger had been incinerated.

Tor lit a cigarette and asked if there was any news. He said he didn't believe the rumours. The Serbs were in the diner every day, they were okay. Had I spoken to them? I shook my head and wondered if they were the three I'd met at the bowling alley earlier in the day.

God knows they might have a motive, said Tor. Those Reservists are bastards when they're drunk. They come here, causing trouble, bothering people, especially foreigners. But you need more than a motive to turn

30

you into a killer, right?

He talked about how they were all bored, the Serbs and the locals. These were lads just like himself. They'd come into the world to work and to fuck. That was all. They'd prepared themselves for it. When they were eighteen or nineteen they would work and fuck. They would use their bodies. Graft and sweat. But there were no jobs here, and hardly any girls. He knew from his own experience what it was like to be unemployed. It drove you crazy. You lost the plot. You lost yourself.

I finished my food and drank up the rest of my beer.

Tor stood up: They're not like you, Robert, you've always been good at writing.

I went to the toilet and vomited. I'd eaten too quickly. The stuff came out in a yellowy-brown gush. Afterwards I bought another beer. I lit a cigarette. That helicopter was still thrumming inside me. The blades were whipping up my insides. I looked at the people walking by in the sunshine. The cars passing. The flash of reflected light. Odda, jittering and shimmering out there.

6

My brother had put on weight. Standing to one side of him I could see his pot belly bulging out over his belt. I'd noticed it before. Frank had filled out. The sight of his little gut under his blue police shirt made me very happy.

The windows in the canteen at the town hall were open, but that didn't help much. The air was heavy, and the room was packed with journalists. They'd appeared from nowhere. Just about every one of them was young, and I guessed that a lot of them were summer temps. All of them were tanned and wearing light clothing.

A couple of them looked familiar from TV, but I didn't know any of them. They seemed to know each other, however. Before the press conference they were standing around chatting and smiling. A blonde girl said they'd lost the way and nearly ended up in Haugesund. A skinny guy with glasses was complaining about the hotel food.

Frank was good. He spoke into the mike in a level voice. I was proud of him. I didn't want my kid brother making a fool of himself

32

in front of a roomful of journalists. He and a detective gave us the facts. The missing person. The search. The discovery. Cause of death unknown. There was nothing new. They talked about the Pedersen kid as if he were an abstract quantity. It occurred to me that a press conference was all about the difficult art of saying nothing in the right way. The police didn't want to give anything away and the press didn't want to show what angle they were going to take.

I'd nodded to Frank when he entered the canteen, but he hadn't acknowledged me. I could see he was nervous. He always brushed his hair back behind one ear when he was nervous. It looked to me as if he'd used too much gel. And as if he was dyeing his hair. In the last year he'd started going grey at the temples. I'd teased him about it.

The press conference was petering out when a journalist from the local paper said something. So far everyone had been following all the rules. They'd just been waiting for the moment when they could get up and start work properly. After the press conference, in the back room or in front of the camera, they could get to work on what really interested them. Maybe they could even get some poor sod to utter the magic word 'murder'.

The guy from *Folkebladet* had never really been much good. You could tell just by looking at him. The big glasses. The bushy hair. The grey beard. He asked if the police were working on the idea that the motive for the murder might be a kind of reverse racism. Silence fell on the town hall canteen. The detective answered that they weren't excluding anything. So far they hadn't formed an opinion on the case. They didn't even know yet if it really was murder.

Old Beardy didn't give up. He asked if the police were afraid a lynch mob might appear in Odda. My brother said no comment. *Folkebladet* wanted to know if the police were concentrating on a particular group of people, if it was correct that the deceased had been observed the previous evening quarrelling with individuals from that group. My brother had no comment on that either. He passed on a request from the family that no pictures of the deceased be published yet. The press conference was brought to a close.

The journalists were grabbing hold of anyone worth interviewing and dragged the detective and Frank along to the court buildings. They got them to pose so that the police sign by the entrance door would be visible in the photo. There were journalists everywhere. I tried to see how many, but lost

34

count. I heard *Aftenposten* ask the detective: when you live in the capital you expect just about anything, but how can something like this happen in a quiet area like Hardanger?

TV2 interviewed my brother. The journalist was young, female, wearing a light trouser suit and sunglasses pushed up on top of her head. I saw my brother brush his hair behind his ear before they started. He tucked his uniform shirt into his trousers in case his stomach could be seen if the camera panned down, and a happy feeling went through me again. Myself, I'd lost weight over the last year, though I was still rotund. We were small and compact in my family, but my weight had gone down. My brother's had gone up. I thought perhaps we'd meet halfway. Maybe it would make me more like Frank. All the same, I felt it gave me a slight edge.

The interview with my brother was over in a couple of minutes. Frank said nothing. He delivered another dose of perfect nothingness. Another TV channel got hold of him and put him on the lawn in front of the foundry monument. Even old Beardy from *Folkebladet* had been pressed up in front of a camera. Are the people of Odda afraid now, TV Norway wanted to know. Beardy was able to confirm it — the people of Odda were afraid now.

I turned and walked over towards the Co-op Megastore. I was going to go back to my office and write up the case. Then home and take a shower. It occurred to me that I hadn't asked a single question. Not that it mattered. You wouldn't get an answer. A press conference was distilled nothingness. You only had to be there. Listen to nothingness. Ask about nothingness. Take a note of nothingness.

I crossed the street and noticed that the man on the pedestrian sign seemed to be disappearing. I hadn't noticed it before; the man in the trilby had become almost invisible. Frank called to me behind my back. I turned and saw him running up the street. I waited. Frank said he'd been speaking to Mum. She was uneasy because Dad had disappeared again. No sign of the old man since early morning. I said he was bound to show up some time. He always showed up. Frank asked if I would call up and see them. He didn't have time himself.

We stood there.

Have you stopped saying hello? I asked.

Frank gave me a look I couldn't fathom. I felt a dizzying jolt inside my skull. The blood pounded in my temples. I noted the cars rolling by along the road. The journalists still swarming round the court buildings. I saw that his uniform shirt was darker under the armpits.

You should change your shirt, I said and turned away.

I walked down the pedestrian precinct. It was just after eight, still warm. There was something restless about the heat, as if the fine weather wanted to be on its way but had been forced to remain. The owner of the Ali Baba kebab shop had taken his TV outside and put it on a white plastic chair. People were watching a repeat of the England game. By the travel agent's boys were playing football against a wall. One of them had great technique. He hit the ball perfectly and it turned into a sun between the houses.

I thought back to the time I played myself. Somewhere at the back of my mind I was still there. The sky above, the mud below. I stopped playing after a knee injury sustained when I was twenty-two. My father had been right. In his opinion I would never have made the top flight. You're too nice, my father had said. Too weak.

Irene had said the same thing at a garden party a couple of years earlier. We sat beneath a parasol, listening to the rain. Are you always this nice? she had asked. We'd drunk a lot, but I remember her expression when she said it. She had never looked at me like that

37

before. I'd held her gaze without answering. For the first time it occurred to me that I couldn't trust myself. I was not a man you could trust.

I went to my office and had a smoke, then looked over my notes. Everything seemed so straightforward. As though a light shone on the case and I could see all the details and the events. As though someone had printed up an X-ray and any fool could see where the disease was. Was it that simple? Had the Pedersen kid been winding up these asylum seekers for a long time, and had they followed him in the Opel and forced him into the river?

I began writing. That was the easiest part of the job. People think a journalist has to be good at writing. A journalist has to be bad in just the right degree. If a journalist ever catches himself thinking that he's going to write well, it's time he was looking for another job. If you want to make a career in journalism, you should be just the right kind of bad writer, or you should quit writing.

An hour later I'd sent off my stuff and lit another cigarette. I rang my parents. There was no answer. I rang again. Still no luck. My father had started this disappearing thing after he got laid off. He would say he was just going into town to buy a paper and then stay out for hours. I'd picked him up in bars, petrol stations, campsites and sports grounds. Usually he'd been sitting there the whole day and read the entire newspaper. In the end someone always calls my brother or me.

The desk rang and said they were going big on the case. They asked me to sex up the opening a bit. I looked over what I had written, and sent off a new introduction. I wondered if I should ring Irene, but decided not to. I should have gone home for a shower but couldn't face it. I played Tripeaks on the computer and won eight hundred dollars.

I sat there until it was nearly ten o'clock. The fan in the computer was whirring away, cooling down the processor. Out in the street I could hear cars passing. Mopeds. Kids. A dog. All the sounds of summer passing by.

7

I went to the car. The wheel was still sticky with blood. I could wash it later. My hand was throbbing, but it didn't hurt so much any more. I drove slowly through the streets, searching the dial for the local radio station. Radio bingo was on. In a monotonous voice the announcer read out a list of numbers. I turned it off again.

The car filled with fresh evening air. It was a little cooler now that the sun had gone down. I lit a cigarette and cruised a bit. On the bridge by the Shell station people had placed flowers and lit candles. Teenagers stood with their arms around each other, sobbing. A TV cameraman standing out in the road told them to move a little closer together.

The picture desk called. They wanted a photo of the boy. I told them that the family didn't want any photos published. The chief replied that editing *Bergens Tidende* wasn't part of the family's job. I promised to try. Back at my office I'd gone through the stock photographs. It was still there. The Pedersen kid with a rifle in his hand. On his face faint traces of orange paint. His head was shaven and the light stubble made the boyish features seem aggressive. There was something scary about him. Maybe it was because I knew he'd just died.

One of the staff photographers had taken that picture. For once I'd been assigned a photographer. We'd followed the gang that played paintball up in the Jordal woods. The photo was never used. The weekend desk had been working on a similar story at the same time without me knowing about it. I'd suggested a double-page spread, but the Bergen version was favoured. On reflection I wasn't too upset about it. There was something twisted about those Reservists. They were a bit too fond of posing in uniform with guns. If the picture had been used they would have got even more excited.

Some kids are allowed to grow up with no guidance, no correction and no interference. People call it mischief. They say they'll grow out of it. They look the other way. And then one day the gang is hanging around the streets and they aren't kids any more. They've turned into something impossible to control. You could see that in the Pedersen kid. It was obvious that he could do something awful. He was capable of doing anything, and he wouldn't have the intelligence to consider what he had done.

The picture desk would have been thrilled to get that picture. But I wasn't going to let them have it. If they hadn't wanted a picture of the boy when he was alive then they weren't going to get one of him now that he was dead. I'd lost track of how many stories I'd written that had never got any further than the internal catalogue. In the past I used to call them up and complain, but I stopped doing that. Nothing ever came of it. I didn't get more stories used because I complained.

At five to ten I parked outside the hospital. I went down the path and over the bridge to Øyna. Here the river split and rushed by on both sides of the lung-shaped island. It was a perfect meeting place. The only people who came here were the bingo players who played in the fishermen's clubhouse on Sundays. At the same time that also made it a dangerous place to be. If someone surprised us it would be hard to explain what we were actually doing there.

The car was hidden among the trees. I sat in the front passenger seat. Irene smoked without looking up. She was wearing a white summer frock. We sat in silence for a few moments. I said something about thinking that she'd stopped smoking. She said she'd started again.

She turned towards me.

I know this isn't the right way, she said.

She stopped. I knew what was coming. I had known it since hearing her voice on the answering machine.

I understand, I said.

Do you?

No, I don't understand.

It was hopeless before, but now . . . There has to be something more. A future. Something like this can't go on without the promise of something better.

I said that nothing was better than this.

She said: Meeting like this? Hiding away? Sitting in a car for half an hour here, half an hour there?

I repeated that nothing was better than this.

It's not that I don't love you, she said. I probably love you more than you know. But this is killing me. It's killing my family. It's killing everyone. That's the difference between us, you see. You've only got yourself to think about.

I said I had her to think about.

Oh, you don't understand.

I've got you to think about . . .

You really don't understand.

I've got you to think about.

Then think about me, Frank!

She broke off. She turned towards me and tried to smile. She'd used my brother's name, as she was bound to have done many times when they quarrelled. Now we were quarrelling, and I could have made something of it. But I didn't.

Finally she said: We can't carry on meeting like this. Not now. Not with all the tension and the police and photographers and journalists all over the place.

Later then? I asked. When things have quietened down?

When things have quietened down?

Yes. When all this fuss is over. Can we meet then?

To do what?

Be together.

We've talked about this before, she said. You mean I should just replace one brother with another?

I said nothing. She was right. It wouldn't work. It was hopeless. I just couldn't bear the thought of letting her go. I said at least we had the same surname. That was bound to make things easier.

She laughed. Then she sobbed.

What have we done, Robert? What have we done?

I put my arm around her shoulder. She pulled away and sat quietly for a few moments. She turned the vanity mirror towards her and wiped her mascara.

We can't see each other any more, she said and sighed.

She took hold of my hand. Only then did she see the bandage: What happened? she asked.

Nothing, I said.

Nothing? Something must have happened.

She took my hand in hers. Then she kissed it.

We sat in silence for a long time.

I'll regret this, she said.

She said she'd regret it when she turned the ignition. She would regret it as she drove over the bridge. When she parked at home. When she went to bed. When she woke up. Every single day she would regret it.

I regret it already, she said.

She kissed my hand again.

This is insane, you realise that? she whispered. What are we going to do, Robert?

I leaned over towards her. She pulled away, like an animal that felt itself threatened. I leaned closer. I ran my fingers through her short, blonde hair. She held my face between her hands and kissed me. I pressed up against her. She resisted, but I wanted to go further. I wanted to get beyond the scent of the perfume and make-up, past what everybody

45

else could smell. And into that which was her alone. Into that which was not mine.

Oh Robert, she whispered.

She opened herself to me. Closed her eyes and put a hand around my neck. She kissed me. I could feel her breath, her heat, the smell that only my brother and I knew. I thought that everything would work out all right.

Abruptly she pulled herself free.

I'm too old for this, she said.

She pulled down her frock and stared up into the vanity mirror. She said she had to go home. The kids were on their own. I turned away. It was dusk. Through the side window I could hear the rushing river. The Opo ran white between the tree trunks in the evening light. The glacial waters nagged and nagged away at the river bank. I thought that if we sat in that car for a hundred years perhaps the river would wash us away.

She said: We can't see each other any more, Robert.

8

I didn't cry. I couldn't even manage to do that. I sat in the Volvo outside the hospital and listened to the radio. Waiting for her to call me. Waiting for her to change her mind. Waiting for her to regret it. She always changed her mind. She always regretted it.

This time she didn't regret it.

Martinsen called. He offered to buy me a beer at the hotel. He said he was disappointed in his colleagues. They were too young and respectable. I drove slowly into the centre of town, thinking that I liked Martinsen. He was the type of man that was always on the go, a man who would drop down dead if he had to stop. He knew where he wanted to go. Maybe that was the difference between a journalist and someone who thought he was a journalist. The instinct. The drive. The code he'd cracked.

I'd read Weegee's autobiography, the first genuine tabloid photographer. He slept with his clothes on, had a police radio in his car, and his arm itched whenever something happened. With a hat on his head and a cigar in his mouth he trawled the streets of New

York looking for fresh corpses. Often he was at the scene of the crime before the police. His torch lit up the back streets. In the morning Weegee sold his pictures of murders and accidents to whichever evening paper made the best offer.

The customers in the Låtefoss Bar looked up when I came in, as if I was the man who was going to save the day. When they saw it was only me they stared back down into their glasses again. It was a quiet evening in Odda. Every evening in Odda was quiet. Odda was like Memphis after Elvis.

Is there a lynching mood? I asked Martinsen.

He was sitting in the bar with a journalist from *Aftenposten* whom he evidently knew. The guy introduced himself. *Aftenposten* asked if I thought it was murder. I shrugged. *Aftenposten* said he thought it had to be murder. He sniggered and said he needed it to be a murder. Nothing had happened for weeks. He was tired of sitting at a desk making routine calls. It was actually unusual. *Aftenposten* said he'd been reporting crime for more than twenty years and there was usually so much shit going on that he hardly had time to finish one case before he had to rush off to cover the next.

I drank quickly. One of the local drunks

turned up; he had a thing about *Aftenposten*.

You don't have a journalist's face, the drunk mumbled. You've got the face of a true friend.

Aftenposten laughed.

Towards midnight the bartender turned up the television. There was a report from the press conference earlier in the evening. I saw my brother and the detective. Briefly I saw the journalists and photographers in the canteen at the court buildings. I saw myself in the background. I looked quite normal. I might have been anybody.

The drunk had climbed up on to a bar stool and was talking about the immigrants, the way they were spoon fed. What about the man who made this country? What did he get? What the fuck did he get?

Made this country? said the bartender. You've done nothing but sit up on that bar stool ever since the sixties.

We joined the other journalists. The guy from the National Press Bureau was in the middle of a story about Sarajevo. He said he'd just been thrown into it. It was like . . . hey, anyone fancy going to Sarajevo? And it just happened to be my weekend off. And, like an idiot, I stuck my hand in the air before I had time to think about it.

The others laughed. The NPB guy rubbed

a hand over his shaven head. He said as they had been driving down Marshal Tito Road in a pickup Serb militiamen had started peppering the car. Those jokers shot at anything and everything.

You don't think, said the NPB guy. You just hide behind the biggest, fattest man around. Right then that was Scherven from *VG*.

Everyone laughed.

Maybe he's on a diet now, but right then I was bloody glad he was carrying all those extra pounds.

Were you scared? asked TV Norge.

You've got no fucking time to be scared, answered NPB. But you have to stay a bit on edge all the time, or else you'll be in trouble.

The Odda drunk was standing at our table. He rolled a cigarette as he swayed from side to side. He lit up and closed his eyes and sang: *You look wonderful tonight.*

I'd drunk five beers, but I still felt sober. Usually that many beers would have me pissing a river, but that evening the beer just sweated out through my pores. Actually it was daylight robbery. You put your money down on the counter, you got your beer, and then the whole thing evaporated into thin air.

I drove home. The streetlights were on, but the June darkness was just something blue suspended between the houses. One day I'd be caught. One day some whistleblower would snitch on me and they'd be waiting for me with a broad grin. So far Frank had told me about all the drink-driving checks in the area. First off I thought he was doing it to help me. Later on I realised he was doing it for his own good — a cop can't have a brother doing time.

Out by Tokheim I turned off the engine. I sat in the car. Through the front windscreen I looked into Odda. The yellow McDonald's M revolved above the bus station. On the spit of land below the zinc factory glinted like a jewel. A few cars were on their way out of the fjord. I followed the lights along the road. I was a fool to love her. A fool to want her. I wanted her to ring. I wanted to hear her say she'd changed her mind, that it was me she wanted.

I remembered the first time she had had to choose between the Bell brothers. We'd been eyeing up the same girl all that New Year's Eve. Sometime after midnight we'd both got up, crossed the floor together and stopped in front of her. She had laughed and looked from one to the other. Then she'd chosen Frank, looking at me with a little smile: Sorry, I chose him.

Some years later, after we'd made love, I asked her about that New Year's Eve. She didn't remember much. She had a bad memory and no sense of direction. I'd asked her what she thought might have happened if she'd chosen differently that night. Only Aunt Augusta knows that, she answered, and kissed my neck. Who? I'd asked. Aunt Augusta, she'd laughed. Aunt Augusta knows everything.

I envied her. She remembered nothing. I remembered everything. I carried the whole damn filing cabinet with me. Every single drawer. Every last folder. I could produce any one of them on demand. Her movements that first evening. The smile when she chose Frank. Her dress. My brother's suit. The dance steps. My coat. The smell of cigarette smoke. The rain as I went out into the night. The first day of the new year.

I let myself in. From the floor above I heard the thump of bass and shouting. The melancholy sounds of yet another failed mini-party. I thought that summer really couldn't be trusted. Over on the desk the little light on the answering machine was blinking. I listened to the messages. One was from Martinsen, offering to buy me that beer. Another was my mother, telling me my father had come home.

I showered. The long day ran off me and disappeared down through the plughole. I dried myself and looked in the mirror. One night I'd told Irene I was too fat. You know what? She'd answered, you're lovely. She'd put her arms round me and told me I was the loveliest man in the world.

I thought of a couple I'd seen kissing in the car park by the church. A soft light falling on them. The sight had turned me on and given me a sense of sinking. I'd stood with my cock in my hand and whispered that she mustn't leave me. Don't leave me, I'd whispered, holding my cock. Don't leave me.

I'd told her that I used to talk to her even when she wasn't there. I talked about stuff that had happened during the day. What I'd done, what I'd thought, what I'd dreamt about. I talked to her about all of it.

Is that normal? she'd asked.

9

I woke to a persistent ringing. The racket made me think whoever it was must have been standing outside for some time. I pulled on some trousers and went to open up. The woman from the neighbouring flat stood on the steps. I saw she had a small cut over one eye. She said: Can I come in?

I was only half-awake but I opened the door. Mumuki slipped past me. I caught a waft of perfume and shampoo. She was wearing a white blouse outside a black skirt. Her dark hair was gathered in a little bun. Mumuki stood there with her arms wrapped around her, as though it was cold and she hadn't dressed properly. From the floor above I heard music, stamping and shouts.

What's the matter? I asked.

Before she could answer the doorbell rang again. Someone was ringing the bell and trying as hard as they could to break down the door. Mumuki didn't say a word. I told her to go into the living room.

Four of the Reservist guys stood outside. I recognised a couple of them from working on the paintball story. I'd seen the others hanging around in Odda. They played the horses, ate fried chicken and generally bad-mouthed people.

We know she's in here, one guy said.

Who? I asked.

We know you've got her in here, he said again.

There's no one else in here.

There's no one else in here, the guy mimicked.

They sniggered and asked me to let them in. The tallest of them stepped forward a couple of paces. I stood my ground in the middle of the doorway. The guy had bleached hair and a tobacco-chewer's pout. He came right up to me and stuck his finger into my chest. A shove from behind made me step to one side. I lost my footing and fell backwards, hitting my head on the floor. The boys were on me. Someone punched me in the stomach, winding me. I curled up into a ball and waited for the next one.

It never came.

I looked up and saw my neighbour. Ask was standing behind the boys. He was a big, powerfully-built man; he grabbed the tallest and pushed him away.

Easy now, said Ask. We don't want any trouble here.

The guy with the lip patted his blond hair

into place. He told Ask that his wife was in my flat.

Ask turned towards me.

Is she? he asked.

I tried to stand up. My body was aching.

You all right? said Ask.

I nodded.

Is she here?

I shook my head.

She's in there! said Tobacco Lip.

Was there anything else? I asked.

Sorry about this, said Ask.

He told the boys to go back upstairs with him. They protested. Tobacco Lip repeated that Ask's wife was in the flat.

I closed the door and went back inside. Mumuki was sitting on the sofa.

Did they beat you up? she asked.

I didn't reply.

I'm so sorry, she said.

I said not to worry. She wasn't the one who'd hit me. I put a shirt on and asked Mumuki if she wanted something to drink. Without waiting for her answer I fetched a bottle of whisky and two glasses. We drank in silence. From the floor above we heard the music being turned up even louder.

I gestured to the cut above Mumuki's eye.

Should I call the police?

No, she said. Please, no police.

Mumuki emptied her glass and asked for a refill. I got up and poured her another. Her slender hands cupped the glass. She said it was good. She'd only been here about three or four years but already spoke almost perfect Norwegian.

It's because of that boy, said Mumuki. The one they forced into the river.

What about him?

It's always like that. People need someone to take it out on.

It should have occurred to me. These guys were friends of the dead boy. They were angry. They wanted someone to beat up. I couldn't quite understand what they were doing in my neighbour's place, but Ask was the kind of guy who would invite anybody home with him. Mumuki asked if I knew what had happened to the boy. I said it wasn't clear what happened to him before he ended up in the river.

The doorbell rang again. We sat in silence. A bottle or a glass broke outside. I thought they might come bursting in, but nothing else happened. It was quiet in the flat above too.

I poured more whisky.

You're a kind man, said Mumuki.

She stood up and walked over to the bookshelves, looking at the books, opening one or two of them. She said my place was a lot nicer than she'd imagined. She thought all men were untidy.

I love reading, she said. You do too, don't you?

She took *Norwegian Wood* down from the shelf and smiled.

Don't you love this book?

I looked at her. It seemed strange. Here was a woman who loved Haruki Murakami, dressed well, yet lived with a guy you could bet had never opened a book in his life. I knew what they said about Ask, but I liked the guy. He used to be the goalkeeper for Odda, retired a couple of years before I played my first game for the team. He made some fantastic saves, but let in some unbelievably soft goals too. Now he worked on the garbage truck, drank in the cheap bars in Odda and had the most beautiful wife in the world.

Can I sleep on the sofa? Mumuki asked.

Is that a good idea? I asked.

Better than going back up there again.

I said she could use my bed. I fetched clean bed linen and changed the sheets. It was difficult with my bad hand but Mumuki helped me. I said goodnight. She stood in the door-way a moment, then turned and closed the door. I switched on the TV. My body was still aching from the punch, and I wouldn't get much sleep anyway. I zapped my way to an old film, something about a train tearing across the desert. A man in a hat and a dark suit got off at some remote station. He looked like Spencer Tracy. He stood on a platform in the desert, obviously with no idea what he was doing there. The local telegraph operator asked him what he wanted. Spencer Tracy said he was only going to be around for about twenty-four hours. The telegraphist said that in a place like that it could feel more like a lifetime.

The doorbell rang again. I stayed where I was. I heard the ringing and then loud voices that disappeared after a while. I got up from the sofa and went into the bedroom to see if Mumuki was all right. Her face glowed faintly in the light from the street. Half her body lay uncovered by the duvet. She slept quietly, still clutching *Norwegian Wood*.

I found a pack of cigarettes in the drawer of the bedside table, put one in my mouth but didn't light up. I wondered when was the last time I had had a woman lying in my bed. I thought of Irene. Now she was lying in the same bed as my brother. It was a picture I tried to keep out of my head, but it kept on coming back. I tried to imagine Irene alone, Irene and me together, but the images were always forced aside by one in which she lay curled up against my brother.

10

Sunlight came slanting between the curtains. It must have been ten or ten-thirty. The phone rang. I was about to answer, but the ringing stopped before I was on my feet. I was sweating like a pig. My body ached. I thought of Irene. Every morning was the same. I woke up and thought of Irene. Sometimes I woke with the feeling that she'd been pumped out of me in the night. I could go and meet the day a free man. Then straightaway she came pouring back and filled me up again. It was as if there was a crack I could never repair.

Good morning, fool! I said to the mirror in the bathroom.

I showered and dressed. I felt a stabbing pain in my left hand. I wondered if the cut had gone septic. I knocked on the bedroom door. No answer. Mumuki had made the bed and left. All that was left was the novel on the pillow. I wondered what would happen to her. I wished she had still been there, that I could have woken her and asked if there was anything I could do. But I had more than enough on my own plate. I picked up

Norwegian Wood and returned it to the bookshelf.

I took the newspaper in from the stairs. Those sick bastards had covered the front page with a picture of two half-naked girls cooling off in the jet from a garden hose. The headline read: *And the heat goes on.* My story was in one of the box columns on the side of the page. Inside they'd given me almost a whole page. They'd used a picture from the mouth of the river. It was a good spread, but they were really sick. I'd ring them up and tell them what I thought of them. Give them a lecture.

The phone rang again. This time I picked it up.

Good morning, said the desk editor.

I didn't answer.

Is it a good morning? she asked.

Yes, isn't it? I said.

She asked if I'd got out of the wrong side of the bed. She said she'd tried to be a bit more thoughtful. She'd learned that at a leadership course. You should always try to do what you've been taught, she said. I asked what she did when that didn't work out. She said that was the next course. Then silence. At a garden party a few years ago she'd come on to me. That was before she began moving up through the ranks. Now she wouldn't dream of it with someone like me. I'd sunk like lead through the system. She'd soared upwards.

We missed you at the telephone conference earlier today, she said.

That bad?

Listen, we're sending you a journalist today.

I thought she might just as well have given it to me straight. She must have attended some course or other where they were taught that. She could just have said that I wasn't up to it. That I was no good. They didn't trust me. They thought I needed backup.

Who's coming? I asked.

Erik Bodd, she answered. Can you pick him up at twelve o'clock?

I didn't answer.

You're an angel, she said.

I had breakfast and drove into town. The sun burned the mountainsides, the pavements and streets. Odda lay spread out like a sheet of white paper beyond the windscreen. Another hot day, another sweaty day. It was getting boring, like episodes of a soap opera.

Fragments of a dream floated up. I couldn't recall it when I woke up, but now I remembered standing at a crossroads up to my waist in water. My father had come down the street in the old Volvo PV. Frank was in the passenger seat. They must have seen me, but all the same they disappeared up a side street. My brother turned round and stared at me through the rear windscreen. The cold water closed in around me.

I bought the tabloids at the kiosk. The woman asked if there was anything new. I answered that I didn't know. She said she thought it must have been the asylum seekers. There'd been so much trouble with them.

What kind of trouble? I asked.

Shoplifting.

Shoplifting?

Yes. Shoplifting and things.

I went to my office. It was in a seventies building they called Founders House. *Bergens Tidende* had been given office space as part of a big initiative. Newspapers, architects and advertising agencies were supposed to get going in Founders House and build the new Odda. Up on the roof now was a huge fluorescent bowling ball. Inside, most of the doors had placards pasted on them: *Office to Let*. The whole of the ground floor was occupied by the Employment Office. They'd moved in when the consultants moved out. Now and then I wondered what had become of all the second career advisers from the Houston Consultancy Group. They used to go round in jeans, reeking of expensive aftershave. In their final report they'd created a model in which Odda ended up classified as 'a dying dog'; either that or 'a sleeping bear'.

I sweated the staircase up to the fourth. The lift had been on strike since the winter. The various owners were still arguing about who was responsible for its maintenance. I checked my e-mails in the hope that Irene might have sent one. I knew she hadn't. She never did, but all the same I entertained the hope each time I checked my e-mails. That was the most pathetic thing about loving someone you could never have. You never gave up hope.

I read the newspapers. Both the tabloids had made the case their lead. *VG* carried a big picture of Guttorm Pedersen on the front page. It looked as if the picture had been taken by a school photographer several years earlier. I wondered how they'd managed to get hold of it. KILLED BECAUSE HE WAS NORWEGIAN? asked the headlines.

Samson Nilsen rang. He apologised for what had happened yesterday. He was only running a business, and *VG* had made him an offer he couldn't refuse. We mustn't take it personally that we hadn't been able to hire a helicopter. He hated not being on good terms with people. Could he make it up to me? He had something that might interest me. He was down on the quays. If I came along he'd give me exclusive rights to what he had.

A few years earlier I had suggested we do a story on Samson Nilsen for the weekend edition. That was when he was still a speedway rider in Poland. Speedway was big over there and Samson Nilsen had become one of the star riders on the Tarnów team. I'd never got a proper reply from the editors of the weekend edition. A couple of weeks later the Sports section went there and did the story.

Samson said that as he was speaking he was standing next to a container full of golf clubs. The putters came from the famous Ping company in Phoenix, and he'd been given the rights to sell them in Scandinavia because he knew the son of the founder. The putters had already revolutionised the game. They had the perfect angle between shaft and head. I half-listened to all this. The guy was a real fount of ideas, but a lot of them were just froth. He'd gone to the local paper with his dream of turning Odda into Golf City. He was going to turn the old factory site into the best golf course in the country. He thought Odda people should do as the Indians had done. In the United States and Canada Indian tribes had opened casinos on a number of reservations so that they could fleece the white man. And with the dollars they earned the Indians bought back more of their own land. Odda people should be thinking along those lines.

I said there was no way I could meet him just now. There was a silence.

You do know I've got something on you? said Samson Nilsen.

I asked him to repeat what he'd just said. Again he said that he had something on me.

Are you threatening me? I asked.

Yes, he said.

I wondered if he knew about Irene. I thought no one knew, but you could never be sure. This was a small town; there were eyes everywhere. Maybe he meant the advertising copy I'd written for him. For long periods of time I had nothing to do at work, and I'd done a couple of small jobs for Samson Nilsen. You could discuss the ethics of it, but then you can discuss the ethics of absolutely anything until you're blue in the face.

Hey, just kidding, said Samson Nilsen.

I waited a few moments before saying that on this occasion unfortunately I couldn't help him. I hung up and rang Martinsen, but he didn't answer. I called Frank, and he didn't answer either. I spoke to the desk sergeant at the police station. Nothing new. No arrests.

I sat a while and did nothing. I needed a

plan or a programme. Ring. Enquire. Note. Investigate. Be annoying. Be a shit. Look like you know what you're doing. I didn't know what to do. Maybe Bergen was right. I needed reinforcements. I needed someone who knew every trick in the book.

I ran my finger over the computer as I rang my parents' house. There was no answer. The finger made a line in the dust. My hands felt warm and pudgy, as though the heat had made them swell. I'd thought the thought many times. Soon there would be a notice on my door too: *Office to Let.*

11

When does something end? When is it really over? It's much easier to know when something begins. Odda, for example, became an industrial town in 1908. Suddenly there it was, the Alby Carbide Union plant, smack in the middle of farming country. But when did it end? Odda had declined so slowly over the last few years that no one could put their finger on it and say: *there* is when it ended.

I remember the first time Irene put her arms around me. We'd got separated from the others in the middle of Lisbon. It was raining, and I'd stopped in front of a shop window to look at some suits I liked the cut of. Irene stood behind me. She leaned up against me, sneaked her arms in under mine and round my chest. I'd glimpsed her face in the window and thought: now it begins.

When was it really over? Irene had ended it so many times that I had lost count. She couldn't take it any more. She couldn't go on like this. Every time she regretted it. It was over, but it never ended. This time I was certain. It was over. Shortly before twelve I drove down to the floating jetty. Ronaldo was there again. He was wearing the same football strip. It was tragi-comic. The shirt told you everything you needed to know about the chances of such a fat boy ever becoming a footballer.

Ronaldo looked up as I walked along the jetty.

They took another one last night, he said.

I turned round and counted the ducklings. He was right. There were only four left. I said we better organise a citizens' patrol. He didn't understand what I meant. I sat down beside him and asked him his name. He didn't reply.

Everyone has the right to be called something, I said. At the very least.

The seaplane approached down the mountain corridor. I'd never met Erik Bodd. He was a recent recruit from the Bergen paper, *Bergensavisen*, where he'd chalked up one big story after another. *Bergens Tidende* had headhunted him to do the same. Now he was one of three full-time crime reporters.

You can see New York from the plane, said Ronaldo. You can see the skyscrapers and all the lights.

I thought he must have flown over Frankfurt on his way here. He must have seen all the tall buildings and thought it was New

York. A few years ago I'd flown over Frankfurt myself and it was quite a sight looking down on all those sky-scrapers in the dark. You sat up there in the plane staring down at office windows that were still lit up. You thought of all the people in those buildings in the evening.

Would you like to live in New York? I asked.

Yes, because they've got McDonald's.

So have we.

But not so many.

Ronaldo looked at me. He said the world wasn't round. I protested, but he wouldn't back down. If the world was round, all the water would just run off it.

You're right, I said. All the water would just run off.

Have you been to New York? Ronaldo asked.

Once, many years ago. Someone took a shot at me with a gun.

What had you done?

Nothing. I was just the wrong man in the wrong street.

Out on the fjord the plane hit the surface of the water and braked. It came buzzing in towards the floating jetty. Ronaldo asked if I had visitors every day. I said it certainly looked that way.

70

My dad's coming soon, said Ronaldo. He's got loads of money.

Without thinking too much about it I'd had a mental picture of Ronaldo with his family. I'd imagined them arguing and shouting at each other. But at least they were together. I asked the boy if he lived with any of his family. He shook his head.

My dad's coming soon. He keeps his money in a shoebox. But that's a secret.

I said that was the smartest place to keep your money. I said I wouldn't tell anyone.

Do you think he'll be able to see me from the plane when he comes?

Definitely.

The seaplane approached the jetty. This time it was the pilot who stepped out on to the float and guided the plane in towards us.

Where did they hit you? asked the boy.

I didn't understand what he meant.

When they shot you, he said. Have you got a bullet in your body?

I explained that they just shot at me. They hit someone else.

Did he die?

I don't know. It looked like it.

I've seen a dead man too.

He didn't say more. I glanced over at him. His cropped hair ended in a cowlick up on top of his head. He had the kind of hair you wanted to reach out and touch.

What's your name? asked Ronaldo.

I fished out my card. I regretted it immediately. He couldn't read. He just looked at the card and handed it back. I said that my name was Robert, and that he could keep the card. Ronaldo pushed it into the pocket of his shorts.

The seaplane had come to a halt. The pilot pulled out something that looked like a golf bag. Erik Bodd stepped out on to the jetty. He was wearing grey trousers and a white shirt. He had tiny sunglasses and gel in his hair. In his left hand he held a suit jacket, and in his right a suitcase. Bodd was dark and tall, but he still looked to me like the kind of guy who'd end up fat. People can have a latent fatness even if they're basically slim. You can see it in the face, the flesh that covers the cheekbones and the forehead, the fat that presses the eyes into their heads.

Behind me Ronaldo shouted: Will you come tomorrow as well?

12

I chatted with the receptionist at the Hardanger Hotel while I waited for Bodd. After half an hour he came down the stairs. The way he snapped his fingers and walked across the floor irritated me.

Did you have to rearrange all the furniture? I asked.

He didn't answer.

D'you know where to find the suspects? he asked.

The suspects?

Yes, the Serbs.

I shrugged. Bodd looked at me.

I want us to understand each other, he said. From now on we're going to be first with everything.

Bodd said we should interview everybody involved. Family. Eyewitnesses. Suspects. The Serbs were probably still in Odda. Anything else would be an indirect admission of guilt. And once they were arrested we should have a photograph of them to hand. And we should also get hold of a photo of the dead boy. *VG* had a picture in today's paper. Why didn't we have a picture?

Should we interview the dead boy too? I smiled.

Bodd rang Martinsen, but got no answer.

Typical, he muttered. Photographers are never there when you need them.

We walked out to the Volvo. Bodd put on his sunglasses and wrinkled his nose as he got into the car. He said he thought at first it was the Odda smell, but it must be something in my car. I wanted to say the smell was better than the stink of his after-shave. But I kept quiet.

We cruised round the hot streets. By Stone Park we passed my father. He was driving a new Volvo. I whistled but he didn't see me. My father had always driven a Volvo. The first was a PV 444 he'd collected from the railway station in Granvin some time in the 1960s. I remember how proud he was when he drove up to our home in that car. My mother immediately christened it 'the Grey Cat.'

I was parched, dying for a beer. As we drove, Erik Bodd explained the way he worked. The first rule was that people lie. People bluff, but you've got to listen. Bodd said that was his strength. He was a good listener. He double-checked and cross-checked, studied what people said. He found witnesses, more witnesses, unknown witnesses. If he was lucky and clever, he'd end up with enough facts to identify the guilty party.

Bodd stayed in the car while I ran in and out of bars, shops and offices. I hadn't a clue where the Serbs might be. If I'd been in their shoes I'd have jumped into the nearest car and put my foot down. Bodd talked about the big *BT* family. He was happy he was finally working for a newspaper with resources. It was years since I'd last heard this kind of crap about the big *BT* family. I thought it had all disappeared after the newspaper went public. But here it was again. Bodd told me he'd cut short his holiday because he wanted this story so much. It wasn't often you got a murder in our area. The story might run for the entire summer.

I found them in the depths of my own building. The bowling alley was about the last place I'd thought of looking, and the first I should have checked. The Serbs were watching the World Cup on a wide screen while they bowled. Italy seemed to be on top, but surprisingly Croatia were winning. The Italians usually kept it pretty tight at the back. Obviously they'd been taken by surprise.

The Serbs had mobile phones they fidgeted with and spun on the table. Their knees were going up and down. It was as if they'd barricaded themselves in down here. I was tempted to tell Erik Bodd that there was no sign of them, but instead went up and said I'd found them.

Bodd rang Martinsen, but got no answer. He swore. We strolled down into the bowling alley and each bought our own coffee. Bodd ordered a Coke as well and told the girl behind the counter he'd come straight from holiday. He needed a real caffeine hit. The girl smiled.

Bodd carried on flirting: If you were selling cool today you'd be a millionaire.

Do you want to play? asked the summer girl.

Let's wait and see, said Bodd. So far the mere sight of you is enough for me to be getting on with.

We sat down. I'd been down here a couple of times before. The foreigners operated in clans. Each one stuck to its own lane. The Serbs bowled on the left, the Kurds in the middle and the Somalis on the right. They played with a silent intensity, as if they had each arranged their own parallel national championship.

I asked Bodd where he'd been on holiday.

Spain, he answered. Costa del Sol.

Good weather?

Thirty degrees every day, he said. Thirty girls every night.

I thought that the desk must have made their decision early yesterday. They'd called Bodd home from his holiday and not said anything to me about it. They'd probably paid for the guy's flight home. They'd paid him to take the story off me. It looked to me as though I had a new job. I was his private chauffeur and his local guide.

We'll try the usual routine, said Bodd. Get in with them, create a good atmosphere, then pump them for everything they know.

After the game he went into the side room. I followed, but stopped in the doorway. Bodd grabbed a seat and sat down in front of the Serbs. He introduced himself in English and said he wanted to know what had happened. He wanted to hear their side of the story. What was true. What were lies. He asked them to speak calmly.

What a prick. He was going to mess everything up. The Serbs made a point of looking straight past him. They stared up at the screen, at the highlights of the match. The Italians had had a goal by Christian Vieri disallowed. The replay showed they were robbed.

So, what really happened? asked Bodd.

Offside, answered one of the Serbs.

They laughed. Bodd laughed.

The good-looking Serb was wearing a New

Jersey basket-ball vest. He leaned over towards Bodd: We've got nothing to hide, he said.

Bodd took out his notebook. What a joker. Pulling out pen and paper was the surest way to make people clam up. Bodd said they should just go ahead and talk. He was a good listener. That was what he was best at. Listening.

No one spoke.

Bodd tapped his pen against the notebook.

I understand how difficult this is. But we're not the police. We're actually on your side.

One of the Serbs asked his mate for a smoke. The pack on the table was empty. Bodd immediately offered one of his.

What do you make of all the talk in Odda? he asked.

No one answered.

It must feel terrible when you're innocent.

The guy in the basketball vest said something in Serb to the others. His mate leaned forward and put a hand on his shoulder, as though to restrain him.

Why should we speak to you? said the pal, the one wearing a red *VG* cap. You won't believe us anyway.

Why not?

Because we're Serbs.

The proprietor of the bowling alley came

78

over and joined in. He was a little guy with a moustache who said that the Pedersen kid had been there that evening. He and his gang had been stirring things up. They always did. It was bad for the place's reputation.

Was there a fight? asked Bodd.

The proprietor shook his head. Bodd turned towards the Serbs and asked: But wasn't there a fight outside Hamburger Heaven? Were you waiting for him? Did you follow him?

Aren't the police supposed to do the investigating? asked the proprietor.

Bodd ignored him and asked if the three of them owned a car. Had they followed the lad and forced him off the road?

He was a snowball, said the guy in the *VG* cap. A potato.

Bodd asked what that meant.

Just that that's what he was, the guy answered. He was a potato.

And that means? asked Bodd.

That he was Norwegian. Like you.

So I'm a potato?

One of the biggest I've seen. There's enough of you to feed a whole family.

Bodd smiled.

Finally the Serb who had been sitting silently alone spoke: If you really want to know, I doubt that any of us will be going to the funeral.

Bodd asked why. The guy wondered if Bodd was deaf.

Bodd didn't give up: why wouldn't they be going to the funeral?

We've got nothing to wear, said the guy in the basketball vest.

The Serbs sniggered. Bodd sniggered too, as though he was one of them. He sniggered and made a note. What a total jerk. I thought the Serbs shouldn't have said anything. But they weren't smart enough to keep their traps shut. They were being wound up, and they hadn't managed to resist. Bodd had things just the way he wanted them.

The best looking one seemed to be the most stupid too.

He said: We don't like funerals. They're so sad. It makes me cry just to think about it.

Bodd looked at me and smiled. He nodded.

So you're the type that's easily moved?

The Serb didn't understand what he meant.

You're very emotional?

Yes, said the Serb. I cry at almost anything.

Bodd asked again what had happened.

No one said anything.

Bodd pulled out his card from his wallet and gave it to the Serb in the *VG* cap. They could call him any hour of the day or night.

Bodd turned and nodded to me. He placed his sun-glasses up on his head and moved towards the stairs. I stayed where I was and watched the TV where they were summing up the match. Christian Vieri lay stretched out on the grass. In his blue strip he looked like a tourist floating in the green water of a swimming pool.

13

Years of experience had taught me that Tuesday after lunch was the perfect time. If I sent my stuff in after lunch on a Tuesday I had a real chance of it getting into print. That was part of working in a regional office — knowing when there were holes that had to be filled with words and pictures.

Now it was Tuesday after lunch and I was squeezing the steering wheel so hard with my hand that it started bleeding again. I should've called Bergen. We've got a loose cannon on board, I should have said. But the ones I got through to would be the same ones that sent the guy. They wouldn't understand what I was getting at.

Erik Bodd sat in the back of the Volvo and snapped his fingers. Everything about the guy irritated me. Some people irritate you from the moment you meet them. The Serbs left the bowling alley just before two. They walked quickly in the direction of the pedestrian precinct while talking on their mobiles. Martinsen took photographs through a wound-down side window.

Walking time bombs, said Bodd.

Martinsen lowered his camera.

Did you get them? asked Bodd.

He said we'd catch up with the Serbs later. Ideally we should have had a team doing proper investigations, but right now the Pedersen family was most important. Where had the boy lived?

You don't interview a grieving family, I protested. You keep well away from a grieving family.

Bodd waited a moment before saying that the victim had a right to be heard as well. It was a principle of law that you should listen to all sides in a case. Since for obvious reasons the lad couldn't speak for himself, the family would have to be his spokesman. I glanced over at Martinsen. He was silent. He was wearing a short-sleeved shirt and sunglasses that hid his eyes.

Bodd leaned forward between the seats: You know this town inside out. We need to use your local knowledge.

I said I could drive them up to Buer. The rest would be up to them. Without wasting any more words I drove up Røldalsvegen, took a right at Vasstun and then straight on across Eidesmoen. Between the trees by the stadium I saw a guy marking the white lines on the football pitch. He moved slowly down one of the long sides. The empty white rectangle reminded me that the team still lacked quite a few players. I'd heard that Odda were having problems putting out a first team this season. Sometimes at the training sessions there were no more than six or seven players. A few local firms had put money in the kitty towards a new goal scorer. A Nigerian had arrived before the season started. He'd scored three goals in the first match and then gone home again. He told the local paper he'd been promised he could go salmon fishing, but the club hadn't got him a fishing licence.

Buer was off the main Odda valley. The rest of Odda looked as if it had lost a boxing match in front of its home crowd, but in Buer valley the glacier had worked unceasingly for thousands of years to create a harmonious U-shape. Later the ice had retreated, as though to admire its own handiwork. Today the valley was full of tourists and grazing sheep.

On Jordal bridge two women and a man sat in canvas chairs in the middle of the road. I braked and pulled over to the side. The man slowly got up. I recognised him. It was the fat guy who had recently taken over the campsite at Hovden.

Åge Lyngstad stuck his head through the window.

Sorry, he said, but the family don't want journalists here.

Bodd opened the door and got out.

We've got an appointment, he said. He was trying it on.

Lyngstad didn't look at Bodd. He motioned for me to get out and drew me to one side: You're a good guy, Bell. But it's tough enough for the family as things are. The press have had the house surrounded all night.

Can't Bell drive in alone? asked Bodd. He's a childhood friend of Pedersen's, after all.

Lyngstad told Bodd to stay away and turned to me again. He said he trusted me. He would see what he could do. He went across to the others. I saw they were having a discussion. One of the women got out a mobile phone. I lit a cigarette and leaned against the hot bonnet.

This is all wrong, I said.

Remember you're a journalist, said Bodd. Not Jesus.

Åge Lyngstad came back. He said Pedersen wanted to talk to me. I could go up to the house alone. I hesitated. Then I put out my cigarette and walked up the gravel path. The little river in the valley was almost up over its banks. It was brown and full of dirt. On the farm were two houses, one from the fifties and a new one I knew Pedersen had had built. The land around the farmhouse had the ragged look characteristic of a farm in decline.

The ice-cream van stood parked outside the house. People said Pedersen had had trouble with the taxman a couple of years ago. That he'd claimed too much mileage against tax. The taxman said he wanted to look at the books, whereupon Pedersen went straight out to his ice-cream van, started it up and drove over to Sweden and back in one weekend.

I went up the steps and rang the front-door bell. I could hear sounds coming from inside. No one opened up. I stood there. I rang again. They couldn't see me from the bridge. I could turn round, have a smoke and then go back. I could say Pedersen refused to talk to us. Forget the whole thing, I could say, forget the whole damn thing.

A young girl opened up. She was wearing a T-shirt with a slogan across her small breasts: I LOVE MY ATTITUDE PROBLEM. The T-shirt couldn't hide the soft swell of her belly above her tracksuit bottoms. I asked to see her father. She half-turned and called out. My eyes were drawn towards her stomach.

Pedersen came out and said hello. He was bare-chested. I said I was sorry to hear about his boy. Pedersen asked me in. I followed him. The living room smelt stale. The TV was on. Another match. Portugal versus Poland in the pouring rain. Pedersen explained that he'd got satellite TV. Now he could choose from six different channels with World Cup football. You could watch the match from the air, from the bench, from the stands. He showed me how. I saw players running round in the kind of rain you only ever see in films.

D'you want a drink? asked Pedersen.

Without waiting for an answer he poured me a vodka. We drank and watched the match. The Portuguese were like Brazil's reserve team. They played entertaining football, and I wanted to support them, but they always disappointed. When the chips were down, they weren't Brazil. I thought it was strange to be watching football in a house in mourning. Pedersen's daughter came in again and sat down on the sofa. She gave me a brazen look. I couldn't keep my eyes off her bare stomach. She noticed and pulled her T-shirt down. Soon it had ridden up again.

Pedersen lit a cigarette and said he'd been meaning to call me. He had a lot he wanted to get off his chest. He stood up and had to take a step to one side to right himself. I smelt the smell of stale booze. I said it was okay if he preferred to wait. Pedersen said he wanted to talk. I repeated that we could wait.

We had time. In such circumstances people often said things they wouldn't normally say.

What are you trying to say? asked Pedersen. Are you saying I've been drinking?

I said that we'd been stopped down by the bridge. They were stopping all the press down there. I said I thought the family wanted to be left alone. Pedersen said he didn't doubt that they meant well. But they had no idea. They didn't know what he'd been through in the last twenty-four hours. No one knew.

I'll speak to them all, said Pedersen. Bring 'em on. Roll up, roll up.

Pedersen's daughter looked at me. I tried to look away. All the time my gaze kept finding that bare stomach. I wondered what it would be like to put my hand on that soft flesh.

You think he was a Nazi, don't you? asked Pedersen.

I don't think anything, I said. All I want is to hear what you think.

You think he was a Nazi. That's what everyone thinks. You're no better than the rest of them.

I said that all I wanted to know was what had actually happened.

He said he smelt a rat here. You come here. Flatter your way in. Play the good friend. All I wanted to do was slander a decent boy.

Maybe his son wasn't Jesus' little sunbeam, but he'd just got himself a steady job.

Do you want to see him? asked Pedersen.

What?

Do you want to see him?

I got up and said I could call back some other time.

Do you want to see him?

I thanked him for the drink and headed for the door. Pedersen stopped me. He grabbed my arm and pulled me towards the stairs.

I want you to see him, said Pedersen.

I tried to shake myself free, but Pedersen had made up his mind. He dragged me up the stairs, one step at a time. I gave up and followed him. A door on the first floor stood ajar. I looked in and saw posters of footballers, a TV, a stereo. I had assumed the boy had been sent for an autopsy, but there he lay, surrounded by flowers. I just caught a glimpse of him and heard someone sob.

Pedersen pushed me up against the corridor wall.

I want you to write that he was a fine lad, he whispered. Guttorm was the best lad in the world. That's what you should write. The best lad in the world.

I heard a woman's voice from inside the room. Someone got up from the bed. Pedersen let go of me and went in. I stayed a moment and heard them quarrelling, then quietly went down the stairs again. The girl was still sitting on the sofa in front of the television.

Out on the grass I lit a cigarette. I walked over to the gravel path and sat on the concrete barrier. I stank. I was sweating. Even my crotch was sweating. A helicopter approached up the valley and began circling above the farm. It came lower and lower until it was no more than thirty metres above the house. Pedersen came out and shouted. He pointed and gesticulated at the helicopter. Clearly he wanted it to land on the grass. I couldn't see why, but then Pedersen tripped and lay motionless on the ground.

I walked down the gravel path. The helicopter climbed and disappeared in the direction of Sandvin lake. At the bridge I greeted the guards. Lyngstad got up from his canvas chair and came padding after me. I didn't turn round. Bodd and Martinsen were waiting down by the Volvo. I said Pedersen didn't want to talk right now. We had no choice but to respect his wishes. The family wanted to wait a while before they said anything. We got into the car and drove slowly into town. I thought of the girl's soft stomach. I thought of the rain falling over a football stadium in Korea.

14

A dog was stretched out in the sun outside the Co-op Megastore. Its back legs were folded underneath it, its forepaws lolling. From the way the dog was lying you could see it was exhausted by the heat. I stroked its head. The dog looked up at me.

I went into the Domus café. Domus had changed its name to Co-op Megastore and now the former Domus café was called City Life. No one called it by its new name, and after they refurbished the place hardly anybody went there either. There were photos of film stars hanging on the walls. James Dean crossing Times Square in the rain. Jean Seberg and Jean-Paul Belmondo sauntering down a boulevard in Paris. Seberg was wearing a T-shirt with *New York Herald Tribune* on it.

From the café you had a view of the electrical goods department and shelves full of toys. Irene and I were standing over there the first time she told me she loved me. It was a gorgeous summer's day the year before last and she was wearing a pair of old-fashioned sunglasses that really suited her. Between the shelves we had spoken of secret things. That was the advantage of falling in love with your sister-in-law; you could chat away to her between the shelves in Domus without arousing suspicion.

I got a cup of coffee and a sweaty bun. Three and a half hours had passed since I'd picked up Erik Bodd at the floating jetty, and already I could hardly stand the guy. Down at the office he clicked his fingers as if he was at the local disco. He said the most important thing was to connect the suspects to the crime, to relate them directly to the killing. That was our job, to find the truth, to get at the cancer beneath the surface.

Bodd's suggestion had been that he and Martinsen stay close to the Serbs. I was to check on the mood in town. The tension in Odda. The air of unreality. The shock. I hadn't protested. Just turned and made my way straight to the café.

Neither the mayor nor the priest answered when I telephoned. I felt heavy and tired. I thought, is there really anything to say about a murder? Someone's dead. Someone's gone for ever. Someone is responsible. Someone must find the person responsible. Is there any more to say? I remembered what Weegee had written in his autobiography. According to him, the easiest case in the world to cover is a murder. There's nothing easier than covering a murder.

I sat a while and watched an elderly couple eating their way through their cream slices in silence. When they'd finished they got up simultaneously, still without a word. It was as though they had no words left any more, but all their movements were coordinated by years of practice. Writing for a newspaper was like that too. You start out with a great heap of words. You write and write. Write about anything and everything. Write early and write late. Write without stopping. Pump out words. Hammer words down. After a while you start to run out. You keep on writing, but you write less and less. You write the same things over and over again, but this time without the spark. Finally there are no words left and you end up just going through the motions.

I went out. At the town hall I took the lift up to the fourth floor. Back in the fifties the town hall had been the pride and joy of the social democrats. The place was meant to be the centre for politics, for admin, for culture. Now there were cracks in the wall, holes in the linoleum, cigarette ends in the pot plants. The mayor's secretary gave me a smile as I went into Reception. She said I could go straight through to Elvestad's office and wait there. He would be along shortly.

The mayor had a miniature putting green in his office. A set of golf clubs was leaning against the walls. A couple of years ago the mayor and I had had a run-in. *BT* had carried several articles about how the Odda town councillors had thrown money away on the stock market. Two of our business journalists had followed the story, but the mayor held me personally responsible all the same. We'd sorted it out later.

Elvestad came in and greeted me. He said he was glad I'd popped in. He'd been thinking of getting in touch himself. He needed a word of advice from someone who knew both the press and Odda from the inside. The whole thing was a tragedy, of course, and he sympathised with the relatives. It should never have happened. It was the first time we'd had this type of trouble in Odda. The council had an emergency plan for situations like this, and so far everything had gone according to it.

But now we have to look to the future, said Elvestad. We need to focus on everything good about this place. Turn the negative into a positive. Isn't that how you see it?

I had no idea what he was talking about.

He said that, for once, Odda was in the spotlight. There were a lot of good journalists in town right now. It was a situation that should be exploited to the full. He didn't know whether to arrange a press conference or approach journalists individually.

I waited. I couldn't see where he was going. Elvestad didn't say any more.

What actually is your message? I asked.

The mayor stood up. He pulled out a handkerchief and wiped the sweat from his face. He said something about Odda being a bit of a backwater. The coast was getting all the attention these days. Great times for the coast. Even though Odda and places like her had brought Norway into the twentieth century she got no thanks for it. He wanted to put Odda on the map again. Accentuate the positive.

The sun had heated the room until it was almost unbearable. I wondered what I should write about the tense atmosphere in Odda. Of course, interviewing the local florist was always a winner. Nothing better than a murder for a florist. Elvestad babbled on about 'encouraging new businesses' and 'being orientated towards problem solving'. It seemed to me he wasn't a bad man. He meant well, and most people had faith in him. He was a folksy man with a natural authority.

I sat there staring at Elvestad's hair. He had

once confided in me that he used to dye it grey. In point of fact he was still quite dark. It was a trick he'd picked up from a book about Bill Clinton. You shouldn't look too good if you want to make a career in politics. In Odda you had to take into account the fact that almost half the voters were pensioners.

I got a text message from Irene: *Ring me at work.*

15

I looked out at the pigeons cooing and mating on the window ledge. The sun was squeezing drops out of my skin, from the inside and out in a continuous stream. I was beginning to lose patience. The mayor was going on about the challenging times that lay ahead for us. The Odda bloke who thought he knew it all didn't know it all; he knew nothing at all, in the mayor's opinion. We had to take with us the best things from the social democratic period and look to the future.

Can you sum up your message in one word? I asked.

The mayor went quiet. He said he was thinking. He wanted to express this just right. He went over to his miniature putting green and played a shot. Then he turned towards me.

If I were to say it in one word, it would have to be: *Up with Odda*.

He said the retraining project had been a success. The report from the Houston Consultancy Group showed as much. A lot of new jobs had been created through the Up with Odda project. Now was the time to get the media involved. I'd already noticed that this was one of his favourite expressions: *get the media involved*. As long as he could get the media involved it really didn't matter much what kind of spin they put on things.

I felt like saying that the report was just playing with numbers. They waved their hands about and made it look as though they'd created new jobs. But most people were doing the same jobs as before, only now they were working for private firms with weird English names. I didn't say anything; I just wanted to get out of his office. I said I'd give it some thought. He'd be hearing from me. Elvestad said he appreciated that.

I went down to Stone Park and called Irene's number. She sighed when she heard it was me. She said she had to hear my voice. She said she had to know if I was okay.

You're not thinking of doing anything silly, are you?

I didn't know what to say. I wasn't sure whether I'd been thinking about doing anything silly or not.

Darling, you mustn't.

I waited. She said she had to see me.

I said she could go over to the window, then she'd see me.

Where are you? she asked.

In Stone Park.

You're kidding.

Go over to the window, I said.

She appeared in one of the library windows. The blinds were down, but I could see she was wearing a light summer dress. She looked round for a few moments before she saw me.

Wave to me, I said.

You're such a baby, she said.

She waved.

She said she was so hot she was about to melt. She said she had to see me. It was probably pretty stupid but she had to. She couldn't bear to finish it like this. Could we meet in the cabin up by the reservoir? One last time?

This evening? I asked.

Yes, she said.

I said I thought I should work, make myself available. You never knew. The police might arrest the Serbs. Someone might go crazy. Anything could happen. All the same this would be a good day to meet her. People had plenty of other things to think about at the moment. We could scratch a little hole in time and disappear through it.

You must, she said. We must.

I wondered how many times it had been like this. I'd thought it was all over. It was never all over. It was over. It carried on. It was over. It wasn't over.

Kiss me, I said.

Suppose someone sees us?

Kiss me.

One look, Robert, and people will know.

Kiss me.

She blew me a kiss.

Shall I pick you up around nine thirty? she asked. Down by the Shell station?

I ended the conversation and remained where I was. It would almost have been better if it was all over. Then I could have sobbed and beaten my head against the ground. Now the body couldn't understand the signals the head was sending out. I was happy she wanted to see me. I was sad because she wouldn't have me.

I could hardly bring myself to stand up. The trees cast shadows across the cobble-stones. Really, Stone Park was nothing special. Just a couple of statues, a few benches, a fountain choked with rubbish and ice-cream wrappers. People only used it on public holidays in May, like May Day and National Day.

I'd always liked it here. Stone Park made me think of other places, far away. Places where you could get up from a bench, walk down a street and vanish.

16

Martinsen rang. They needed a car. I asked why they couldn't hire one. Martinsen said they'd hired a car, but they needed a driver who knew the area. Urgently. I walked slowly over to the Volvo and drove up to the police station. Martinsen and Bodd jumped in. They told me to follow a black Saab which was cruising down Folgefonngata. I asked what was happening.

VG is in the black Saab, Bodd said from the back seat.

I drove along Folgefonngata and was on VG's tail before we reached the main road. Martinsen glanced in the wing mirror.

Dagbladet and NTB are on our heels, he said.

Can you see the police? asked Bodd.

He said they were driving two cars, a white Subaru and a metallic-grey Toyota. I caught sight of the cars some way in front of the Saab. They indicated left and turned on to the main road. We drove in procession up the valley. At Eide the police cars drove around the streets before they turned back the way they had come. They drove slowly so it was easy to tail them. It looked as if they didn't know where they were going.

Where are they actually going? I asked.

Bodd said he had no idea. But when *VG* sat on the police's tail you did the same. No one had better contacts than *VG*. When the police wanted to give a tip-off they always gave it to *VG*. We headed back towards the centre and then out west. I wondered if they were playing with us, if this was some trick. Bodd asked if there were asylum seekers living anywhere else besides the hostel. I said some lived in the centre, but none had been placed out this way.

So what kind of people live out here? asked Bodd.

I live out here, I said.

Damn — are *you* in the frame? Bodd grinned.

At the timber depot by Egne Hjem both police cars slowed down, indicated, then drove up the gravel track to a parking bay beneath the rock face. *VG* followed. So did I. In the rear-view mirror I saw *Dagbladet* and NTB.

We reached the little plateau above the fjord and parked over to one side. Three men and a woman climbed out of the Subaru. Four men got out of the Toyota. Bodd snapped his fingers.

What the hell are they doing here? he asked.

Through the windscreen I saw a man open the boot. He lifted out a black bag and carried it over to one of the tables. The woman followed him. She was carrying a green plastic supermarket bag.

What the fuck are they up to? asked Bodd.

Even old Beardy from *Folkebladet* was here by now. He clambered out of an old Lada. The detective from yesterday's press conference sauntered across the parking place. He came straight over to my Volvo.

What's going on? said Bodd from the back seat.

They're having a pizza, I said.

The special branch guy leaned into the side window.

You guys hungry? he asked.

We didn't answer.

Special Branch said: Because if you're not, then leave us to eat in peace.

He went over to *VG, Dagbladet*, NTB and *Folkebladet*. He bent down at each car and spoke to the journalists. I had been right. There was a pizza in the black bag. The police laid the table and got ready to eat. We sat for a while in silence.

Shit, said Martinsen. Are we going to sit here and watch them eat?

I reversed and we drove back into Odda again. Erik Bodd said watching the detectives eat had made him hungry. He wanted to go to McDonald's. Martinsen refused. As a matter of principle he never ate at McDonald's. Bodd asked when exactly Martinsen had become so high-minded.

I suggested we go to Chinatown. Every self-respecting country town should have a Chinese restaurant, and now Odda had got one. The food there was actually pretty good. No one objected. I parked by the church and we walked to Chinatown, which was on the ground floor of what had formerly been The Happy Corner. The previous owner of the dance club on the first floor had called his place The Hard On without having the slightest idea what 'hard on' meant. Before the place went broke they'd tried karaoke and stripping.

Mumuki stood behind the counter, smiling. Her hair was pinned up and she was wearing a red summer dress with a dragon pattern. I asked if everything had turned out okay with her husband. She thanked me for helping her. I said she only had to ask if there was anything else I could do for her. She nodded and smiled again.

Are you ready for some of the best food in the world? she asked.

Bodd pulled me aside: Something going on here?

We ordered and sat down. At the next table they were having a detailed discussion about the murder. A man in sunglasses was saying that the Pedersen kid must have been killed by someone who knew him. They knew who he was and had followed him that night. It couldn't be random. It had to be someone who knew him. Another guy disagreed. It occurred to me they were discussing the murder the same way they would've discussed a football match.

Above the indoor goldfish pond was a poster showing an aerial view of Odda. There were several photos from the fifties of workmen in working clothes. A caption below read: TOUGH TIMES FADE AWAY. TOUGH GUYS DON'T. An advertising agency in Oslo had come up with the slogan as part of the council's retraining programme after the factory closed down. Rumour said it cost the council three hundred thousand crowns. *Folkebladet* later found out that the slogan had been stolen direct from a similar campaign in Detroit, Michigan.

The desk editor rang just as our food arrived. She wanted me to find out if the Pedersen kid had owned a dog. Apparently someone had tipped them off that he liked Alsatians.

It would give a human-interest twist to the story, she said. The dog that lost its beloved owner.

It certainly would, I said. Do you want me to do a profile of the dog?

Bodd laughed. We ate.

Bodd nodded towards Mumuki behind the counter. He said he'd heard a story about the new editor-in-chief. He'd been to a newspaper conference somewhere in the Far East and on the way back had a stopover in Bangkok. He ran marathons and had some kind of back trouble. He'd visited a massage parlour where he'd had all sorts of oils and lotions applied to him. The massage was getting more and more intimate. He felt uncomfortable but didn't dare say anything. Finally the Thai lady had smiled and said: *Mistha, you want happy ending?*

Bodd chortled: And according to him, before he could even answer, his cock jumped in by itself. That's what the guy said — it just jumped in by itself.

But isn't he a Christian? asked Martinsen.

He's a Personal Christian. He doesn't go to church. And if you're a Personal Christian in Bangkok, then, by God it just jumps in by itself.

Martinsen glanced at his watch. We had to go and check out the protest march. Bodd said he'd been given the go-ahead by the desk editor to identify the Serbs if they got arrested. She'd discussed it with the editor-in-chief and they both agreed. Bodd asked for my opinion. I said I couldn't see the point of identifying them.

No? asked Bodd. Don't you think the Serbs are bastards anyway and it's about time someone said so?

I didn't say anything.

Bodd wondered why I hadn't mentioned that we had the best contact of anyone in the police.

Can't you tickle your brother a bit?

I said I didn't know what he meant.

Tickle him a bit, said Bodd. You know, get him to open up.

Bodd said all was fair in love and journalism.

It won't work, I said.

Why not? asked Bodd.

Because my brother isn't ticklish.

17

Up in Stone Park it struck me that every town in the world must have its quota of idiots. Now Odda's one per cent had gathered to demonstrate. The Reservists were standing over by the fountain. My old gym teacher was slopping around in a shell suit while he rolled himself a cigarette. A man they called the Cunt Snatcher was talking to someone from TV2 and holding up a handwritten placard — *Arrest the Guilty*.

Even so there must have been twice as many journalists as demonstrators. Everyone was chasing round for angles and people to interview. NTB spoke to Hans Petter Matre. NRK concentrated on following Bitter-Egil. Old Beardy from *Folkebladet* jotted down notes as he interviewed Johnny 99.

Someone bellowed through a megaphone and an over-weight guy clambered up on to a white plastic chair. Truls Trondsen was a local member of the Progress Party. I remembered from the time he ran the satellite dish outlet at the Fjord Shopping Centre. Before he went broke he'd installed a dish for me at my place. I was eternally grateful. Now I had fifty-seven channels and nothing worth watching.

Erik Bodd came over and said I could catch up with the demo and the memorial service afterwards. If anything special happened I could write a few lines. Otherwise drop it. This was *VG*'s production. *VG* had asked people to gather to show their anger. *VG* was in charge of the whole thing. They'd even made the demonstrators' placards for them. I asked if he was joking.

Truls Trondsen shouted into the megaphone: no one was to exploit the situation, or the family's grief. All the same, it was fair comment to say enough was enough. The cost of integration was becoming pretty expensive.

The tiny group applauded.

I'd read on the internet that several Progress Party leaders had announced their intention of visiting Odda. None of them were here now. They'd probably chickened out after accusations that they were making political capital out of a tragedy. This was Truls Trondsen's big day. People in Odda called him 'Knickers' from his habit of nicking women's panties from washing lines. He was wearing a dark suit that looked too tight. Sweat beaded on his forehead. Truls Trondsen was a big man with a lot of excess weight to get rid of. I wondered if he was wearing women's panties under his suit.

This was about values, Knickers shouted. It was a battle against every force that challenged our Christian cultural heritage. For over twenty years we'd made no demands of the people who came here. And it was about time to speak up.

After the speech the little procession made its way from Stone Park and down along the pedestrian precinct. People watched from the pavements. There was an air of anticipation, something half-threatening. Knickers marched in front holding a placard: *No Asylum for Criminals.* The other jokers walked along behind him. The tiny procession was ringed by journalists. I couldn't remember the last time I'd seen so many journalists in Odda. Probably not since the time the council hired a professional cat killer from Haugesund because the feral cats were becoming a problem. The cat killer laid traps for them and despatched them with a shot through the back of the neck up in the sand pit. The press had piled into town. I'd followed the hunt along with TV2. On that particular afternoon it had rained and there wasn't a feral cat in sight. TV2 had a seaplane on standby and a deadline to meet. From the back seat the reporter kept saying — *Dammit, we've gotta get a fucking cat!*

We passed the old Lepers Park and it struck me that this was the very place for the press corps. Nearly all of them were scruffily dressed. They were wearing T-shirts and khaki shorts or jeans. One girl had both a sunshade and sunglasses pushed up on top of her head. It looked absolutely ridiculous. Journalists had no style any more. In the forties, for example, Weegee always wore a suit, tie and hat to photograph in. In his book Weegee wrote that you could lose your job, or even your home, but that life without a suit just wasn't worth living.

Down by the church the procession came to a halt. One photographer gave another a shove. *VG* accused *NTB* of deliberately getting in his way. *NTB* accused *VG* of provoking the situation. They were ready to start swinging at each other when their colleagues came between them. The other photographers turned briefly towards the two fighting cocks and clicked away for a few seconds.

I couldn't keep a straight face. I stood there grinning. The whole show was just too absurd. *VG*'s photographer saw me grinning and came over to me. He pushed his face into mine. He had a small moustache and a bald dome on which drops of sweat glistened.

Do we have a problem? *VG* asked.

What kind of problem do you mean?

Do we have a problem?

What sort of problem?

Listen, I ask you a question, you ask me a question back. It's not getting us anywhere. Do we have a problem or do we not have a problem?

No that I know of.

It looks as though we have a problem.

No, we don't.

So there's no problem here?

No problem.

Good. Because for a while here it looked to me as though we had a problem.

No. Absolutely no problem.

That's good. No problem is very good.

VG's photographer stared at me before slowly backing away from me. He nodded and turned round. The demo was still going on down by the river. They lit candles on the quayside and laid wreaths. A helicopter approached from the fjord and hovered over the river mouth. The crowd sang 'God bless our precious fatherland' through the roar. Some of them shook their fists at the helicopter.

I walked back up to the main road and then stopped and stared down towards the quayside. Photographers and journalists circled the little gathering. Lenses and microphones created a kind of energy and electricity. Something appeared in focus. Something became clear. At the same time I had a feeling that the town was vanishing. Odda was becoming invisible. Odda didn't exist any more.

I walked over to the car and drove up towards Hjøllo. The breeze from the open window cooled my head. TV2 had got their cat that time. Half an hour before they had to get back to Bergen the reporter had tricked some little boys into handing over an animal. He told them it had to be taken to the vet. The boys had reluctantly handed the animal over. For the benefit of the reporter the cat was then shot in the back of the neck up in the sand pit.

18

My father's Volvo was parked outside the house, but no one was home. I heard laughter from the basement, popped my head in and saw that an American sitcom was on TV. Somewhere or other I had read that the canned laughter for most of these shows had been pre-recorded back in the fifties and sixties. Every time I saw a sitcom I wondered what people had really been laughing at back then.

A row of family portraits hung on the walls. Photographs of the happy days, the good days that had to be documented so that we could make it through all the other days. A wedding picture of Irene and Frank hung there. I'd made a speech for them that day. I'd even written them a song. There was one picture of Irene on her own. She was a little too heavily made up, but she looked lovely in a white dress. I stared at the picture and wondered whether there was a moment when your life changed direction and would never be the same again, when you're floating in the river and feel the pull of the current for the first time.

My parents were sitting in the shade under the balcony. They were playing radio bingo. There was a clock radio on the garden table. The announcer called the numbers in a sleepy voice. My father had taken off his shirt so that his belly swelled out over his shorts. He'd let himself go after he got laid off. My mother was wearing a blue dress. She was getting smaller and smaller.

How are things? I asked. But my mother just shushed me.

I sat in a garden chair. The sun went down behind the ridge of Eidesnuten. The whole of Hjøllo hissed to the sounds of garden sprinklers and high-pressure hosepipes. The smells of barbecuing wafted up. People sat out in gardens and on balconies. But it was as if they weren't there, as if they had become a part of the landscape.

I noticed how shaggy Odda had become. The place seemed to be swathed in firs. Bushes and trees had grown up round the houses and other buildings. I thought it only a matter of time before nature took over. Odda had once been full of industry and pollution. Now nature was taking its revenge. Even deer had started coming down to Hjøllo. Once my mother tipped me off about a deer that had got into the fruit and veg department at the Rimi supermarket, but by the time I got there the animal had already been killed and carted away.

While I sat there in the garden, the rest of my dream from the night before came back. I remembered that the water had risen almost up to my neck by the time my father finally reversed the car. Without a word I'd clambered into the back seat. We'd driven through Odda in the late evening. We got held up again at Hovden and sat staring up at the lights of the Bruce villa. Slowly the water rose inside the PV.

I went to the bathroom to clean my cut. I wondered if I should shave off my beard. I once asked Irene if she thought I had too much hair on my body. That made her laugh. She was sitting up in bed wearing only a pair of blue panties. I had kissed her breasts. What a question, she had said. I looked at myself in the mirror. There were two men in there. The one I had been, and the one I was going to be for the rest of my life.

I went down into the cellar. It smelt of turpentine and rotten apples. My father kept piles of old newspapers here. He had his own system for what had already been read and what was to be read later. I moved a rowing machine and a table-football game out of the way. I searched through old school reports and football magazines. At the bottom of one box lay some Mother's Day and Father's Day cards. On the shelf I found a Viewmaster with 3-D cards from various Disney films. I held it up to the light and saw Mickey Mouse taking aim at a huge bear with a shotgun.

I was sure Frank had said the letters were hidden here. He had asked me to look after them for him. He hadn't the heart to throw them out, but I had refused. Being his alibi was quite enough. After a trip to Glasgow a few years ago I'd booked into a hotel in Bergen while Frank stayed on for another day. We had to get back to Odda at the same time. Irene mustn't be allowed to see me a day before Frank. The hotel was next to the railway line. I'd watched the trains, read a book, hadn't spoken to anyone. For twenty-four hours I had ceased to exist.

The letters lay between some old note-books in which Frank had drawn scenes from the Bible. I glanced quickly through them, took the letters out to the car with me and placed the bundle in the glove compartment. I would use them if I had to. I was a fool to love Irene, but I wanted her. My brother had taken from me the only thing I had ever loved. One day I would do the same to him.

I drove down to the river. A crane truck on the Hjøllo bridge was trying to winch up the Opel. A TV crew was filming. I parked, got out and joined the other onlookers.

Long time since they landed such a big fish here, said one guy.

And they said the river was dead, said another.

I caught sight of Dean Martini under the bridge. He lived most of the year down by the river. He certainly wouldn't remember it himself, but I'd done a feature about him one weekend. He was a local character. People called him Dean Martini because he was always so elegantly dressed. Now he was sitting in an armchair with a glass in his hand. I should have thought of it before. Dean Martini might have seen something that night.

I walked down the steps by the suspension pillar and said hello. He raised his hand to his forehead and saluted. I said it was warm. He didn't respond. I asked if he wasn't afraid of getting carried away by the water. The heat had caused the water level in the river to rise dangerously over the last few days. The experts were afraid there was going to be a repetition of the floods of the fifties.

How long have you been a cop? asked Dean Martini.

He clearly didn't remember me.

I'm not a cop, I said.

You are a cop. I can tell it a mile off.

Then where's my uniform?

Plain clothes.

I work for a newspaper. I'm a journalist.

That's what I said. Plain clothes.

I asked if he'd been down here on Monday night. Had he seen or heard anything when the car went into the river. He replied that he'd had a few drinks that night. He explained that he drank to keep his bodily fluids in balance. That was the only reason he drank. He was keen on keeping his bodily fluids balanced. It was quite a job.

You've got to work at it and keep working at it. The fluid balance has to be perfect. If you suddenly lose it you find yourself in all sorts of trouble.

He said that was his job. To keep his bodily fluids in good order. At the moment he had a little time off, but sometimes he'd worked on his days off too. He raised his glass. I said I didn't doubt that he had the toughest job in the world. I turned and started to walk back towards the steps.

Dean Martini called after me: Hey you — Lobby Ludd!

I stopped.

How much is my memory worth, do you reckon?

I shrugged and walked back.

Shall I tell you something about this river?

119

he asked. Something you didn't know? Something secret?

He paused for a long while.

This river is a bear, said Dean Martini. Understand? This river is a floating bear.

He leaned in towards me, as if he were going to tell me a secret.

This river sleeps in the winter, he said. And then wakes up again in the spring. And then the river is treacherous. Small boys shouldn't come here with their shrimping nets. Little boys will get eaten up by the river in spring.

I thanked him. I told him it was the best tip-off I'd had for a long time.

So where's my money? he said.

I said I didn't have any money on me. If he came along to the office, he'd get paid. I walked slowly back to the steps again.

Bloody copper! Dean Martini shouted after me.

19

I got into the car and drove down Røldalsvegen. Journalists milled around outside the courthouse. Some combed their hair. Some put on make-up. Everyone was using mobile phones and peering into camera lenses. It occurred to me that they looked as though they were working on a production line, as though the production process had been moved out here from the abandoned foundry.

I braked and pulled over. Frank came out on to the steps. He was wearing his aviator's shades but took them off when he got a microphone stuck in his face. He didn't see me. The blonde girl from TV2 was doing aerobics on a soft drinks crate. A photographer took aim. There was a radio car next to him with a dish on the roof and a slogan on one side: *Being There*.

Bodd called. I'd assumed he'd be at the press conference, but he asked me to come out to the industrial estate at Eitrheim. He said he'd made an interesting discovery. I looked at my watch and wondered if this would spoil my chances of meeting Irene.

I sat there a while longer and watched the gathering. The reporters' faces were strangely set. As though they were trying to reflect the case they were reporting. As though they really cared, and this place meant something special to them. Next week you might see them reporting from somewhere completely different. They might be doing a live broadcast that required smiles and one-liners.

I drove out towards Eitrheim. At the parking lot next to the vehicle licensing centre a group of people were attending a dog-training class. The dogs ran in a weird pattern round some cones while their owners whistled to them. The area north of Zinken was half wasteland. There was a car salvage business and several other small concerns that still hadn't gone bust because of all the millions put into regenerating the town. Once the council had housed alcoholics in temporary accommodation out here, but they refused to live so far away from the drinking shops in the centre. They got together, lobbied and forced the council to give way. Now the temporary accommodation was right next to the church.

Martinsen and Bodd were standing by the burnt-out wreck of a car down by the jetty. Bodd nodded to me and said it was a BMW, or what was left of one. The car was so badly damaged I didn't see how anyone could work out what make it was. But I didn't ask. I couldn't bear the thought of hearing Bodd going on about investigative techniques again.

Who gave you the tip-off? I asked.

Doesn't matter who, answered Bodd.

He said this might well be a breakthrough in the case. We might well be the only ones working on this clue. It was a dead cert front-page story.

I did a bit of checking round, said Bodd. The Serbs did actually have a car.

What kind of car? I asked.

Give you one guess, said Bodd.

I congratulated him and thought it was damn strange to dump a car here and then set fire to it. If you want to get rid of a car in Odda, you've got the whole of South Fjord at your disposal.

Bodd and I agreed what I should write about. I made my way to my office and wrote as fast as I could. The new editor-in-chief had said at an in-house seminar that we shouldn't write too much long-winded stuff in *BT*. Readers were getting stressed because they couldn't take in everything that was being written in the papers. We had to give them a chance to relate to as many stories as possible. Ideally it should be possible for a reader to get through the entire paper while sitting on the toilet. That gave them a good 'newspaper experience'.

At nine I made my way home to change and have a wash. I was looking forward to seeing Irene. I wanted to put my arms around her. That was all I wanted to do. Put my arms around her. Be with her. I buttoned my shirt slowly and watched some boxing on one of the sports channels. A black man was hammering away at a white man. They looked like two guys picked up off the street to fight before the main event of the evening.

The black man stumbled. He was clearly an amateur. The lack of boxing skills made the fight even cruder. This was pure aggression. Just two men fighting between ropes in a brilliantly lit ring. Finally they stood there just holding on to one another, like some desperate married couple involved in a sick act of love.

In the Weegee book I had been reading about a title fight in the forties. The photographer had worked out that it would be difficult to get his pictures back to the office in time, so he hired a private ambulance and driver and hid inside it. After taking a few shots of the boxers he ran out to the ambulance and drove back to the newspaper offices, with the siren on and the blue light flashing. The police cleared the road as Weegee lay on the floor and developed his negatives.

The phone rang. A man asked if I had looked at the video. I'd heard the voice before, but I couldn't place it. The voice had been jolted out of context and I just couldn't quite get it back in again.

Again the man asked if I had watched the video.

Who is this?

Check your mail.

Who am I talking to?

There was a click. I stood there a moment. The post was out in the hall. I'd taken it in without going through it all. Among all the junk mail and the bills I found a brown Jiffy bag. There was no stamp on it. Someone must have pushed it straight through the letter box. My name was printed on a label. Inside was a video cassette.

I pushed it into the player and sat down to watch. It was a grainy, amateur recording, made at night. Through wire netting I could just make out trailers and trucks beneath street lamps. A sudden rain shower showed up in the light. The trucks drove back and forth inside what looked like an industrial estate. The first part of the recording was made from a distance. Then there were diffuse close-ups of pipes, machines and instrument panels. The film lasted about ten or twelve minutes. I rewound it to take another look. I got nothing out of it. The video was a fluid smudge of shifting greys. Most of it was out of focus. I noted the date and time. The recording had been made one night in April.

As I dressed I tried to place the voice from the telephone. I still couldn't. It was as if I was on a quiz show where I knew the answer but couldn't locate it in my memory.

20

Shortly before ten we drove through the Tyssedal tunnel, turned off towards Skjeggedal and went off the map. I was calmer. If anyone was on to us, we would have realised it by now. I'd sent in two stories to the paper as well as keeping Erik Bodd posted about how things were looking.

The Volkswagen hummed along the road. The roof of the cabriolet was down and the wind tugged at Irene's blonde hair. She kept up a good speed along the narrow gravel lane. She was a good driver. When we rounded the final bend and could see the cabin in the twilight, she took my hand.

Shall we go for a walk before? she asked.

Before what?

You know.

The last rays of the sun had licked the mountain tops and vanished. The air in the valley turned chillier. We walked across the Ringedal dam. Irene was talking about something that had happened at work. I listened but didn't speak much. I was just enjoying her closeness. She had changed and was wearing a blue dress with flowers on it.

The reservoir had almost been emptied. Dealers had been selling off the power to foreign buyers and I'd received an anonymous tip-off that the company was illegally tapping the water. They took most from the reserve when electricity prices were high, and when prices fell they bought their power cheap from coal-fired stations on the Continent. It meant they could pump water up into the higher basin and sell it off again the next time prices peaked. I'd tried to raise interest in the story, but without success. Even head office weren't especially supportive. They said the source was suspect and decided that it would cost too much to fund a full investigation of any possible illegalities in the tapping.

My grandfather had worked on the Ringedal dam. He'd travelled from Sunnfjord to Hardanger to get the job. I'd seen pictures of him in working clothes and a flat hat posing with the other workers. He resembled my father in those pictures.

Irene held my hand again. That was perhaps the best thing of all. To walk hand in hand with her. Something so simple and yet so hard. From up on the dam we could look down at the VW Beetle and the cabin. From up here it looked as if people were on an innocent little holiday at their cabin. They sat down there and everything was idyllic. Maybe they were playing cards and listening to the radio. Each time we met here I imagined the dam bursting and all the water flooding down and carrying the cabin and the car down towards the fjord at terrific speed.

I asked Irene why she wanted to see me again. I was afraid to ask. I was afraid of forcing her into something final, something which did not include me.

She stopped and put her arms around me.

I don't have a choice any more, Robert. It's way past that now.

Above us a plane headed west. In the pale evening light I could see the lights blinking under the fuselage. I thought of the passengers in seats up there. Reading maybe, yawning, glancing down at the rugged landscape below.

I asked if she remembered the film where two lovers talked about what they would take with them if they had to go away. She didn't remember it. I knew that she'd seen it, but she never remembered anything.

What would you take? I asked.

If I had to go away for ever?

Yes.

I would take my books. Some records. Nothing more. I don't need that much.

I waited. I said that I would take everything

with me. The lot. She laughed and said that in that case I might just as well stay. Because if I went away for ever, I would miss everything. I would have to take the house I lived in with me. The Volvo. My street. The whole of Odda.

She pressed her cheek to mine.

If I left, I'd have to take you with me, she said.

Would you?

Yes, didn't you hear what I said? I don't have a choice any more, Robert.

We strolled down to the cabin. As we walked, she leaned her head against my shoulder. Inside I opened a bottle of wine. She sat on the sofa and sipped from her glass. We talked about everyday things. I sat in a chair opposite her. I just wanted to stand up and put my arms around her. But I also wanted the moment to last.

What are you thinking about? I asked.

I'm not telling you, she answered.

I wondered whether I should show her the letters. I'd taken them with me and put them in the glove compartment of the VW. But I wasn't sure how she would react if she read them. All I wanted now was to be here with her.

I couldn't wait any longer. I walked over to her and laid my head in her lap. She stroked my hair. I pressed my face into her stomach.

She wrapped her arms around me and said: How d'you think it would have worked out if it had been us?

Badly, I said.

Badly.

Yes. I love you too much.

Is it possible to love someone too much?

Yes. You wouldn't have liked it. It would have bored you to death.

It's good to be loved. No man has ever loved me like you do.

But it's exhausting after a while.

She laughed and kissed me.

Come on, let's go to bed.

She took me by the hand and led me up to the bedroom.

She undressed quickly and sat naked on the bedside. She followed me with her eyes as I took off all my clothes. She used to tease me about the neat way I laid my clothes down after I undressed. No way could I be a good lover. I walked over to her and held her. She was warm. I felt her breath on my face.

Now I can tell you what I was thinking of, she said.

And she pulled me down over her.

This is what I was thinking of, she whispered.

21

I awoke to the sound of a chainsaw. A dog howling. The sounds drifted and spread down over the valley, were tossed back and forth between the mountainsides. Irene was gone. The VW was no longer outside the cabin. I looked around for a note with some kind of message. I wondered if maybe she'd just driven off to buy some breakfast.

I went into the bathroom to wash my face. The smell of Irene lingered on my fingers. The night was still in me, as though Irene surrounded me even when she wasn't there. I had looked forward to waking up with her. Holding her while she was still somewhere between sleep and the new day.

It was ten o'clock. The heat began to creep into the cabin. I went outside for a smoke. I didn't know what to do. There was no network coverage there and I should have been at the office by now. Bodd was sure to be annoyed with me. The desk editor would give me a ticking-off.

I waited half an hour before I walked down the gravel track. My footsteps were light and slow. It occurred to me that making love has a delayed reaction. You touch the skin of the woman you love, and everything is as it should be. But you can't take in all the caresses. They flow over you some hours later, like a soft aftershock.

I had woken in the middle of the night and reached out for her. She had received me, more calmly, with less hunger. She had put her fingers into my mouth and made me kiss them. Then she had stroked them over my skin. In the first light I had sensed the wetness drying.

I heard an engine behind me. The garbage truck came rumbling down the track. I thought about hiding, but they must have seen me already. I stopped by the side of the road. The driver stuck his head out of the window. It was my neighbour.

Good morning, Ask grinned.

His mate opened the door for me and I jumped in.

Killed anyone up there? asked Ask.

I tried to smile.

Hope you didn't dump the body in the reservoir. They sell the power off so fast they'll find the body before the summer's over.

I said I was working on a story. It was a stupid thing to say, but I really didn't know what else I could have said. Ask laughed and chewed gum.

133

We're working on one too, he said and gave his partner a nudge. Isn't that right, Georg?

Ask whistled tunelessly. We came into an area where the mobile picked up a signal again. Last night's messages came clicking in.

Is it about a woman? said Ask.

His partner sniggered. He was a small, red-headed guy who I seemed to recognise from somewhere out in the fjord. Ask said I didn't have to answer.

It's always about a woman when an unshaven guy shows up in Skjeggedal, he said. Never fails. I don't blame you. You're single. You're okay looking. Just get it where you can.

Ask said just recently he'd been thinking a lot about getting himself a black one. Damn it, he'd never had a black one.

Wouldn't you fancy a black one? he asked me.

Georg sniggered.

Ask looked across at Georg.

You've had a black one, Georg. You bugger, you've had a black one.

Georg just sniggered again.

Imagine going through your entire life and never having it with a black, said Ask. You're lying there in the old people's home and some journalist from *Folkebladet* turns up and asks if there's anything in your life you regret. And you've got to own up — you'd have loved to have had a black one.

We reached the edge of the mountainside and the valley opened out. Beneath us we could see Tyssedal, the fjord and the factory. Smoke rose from the chimneys at TTI, where the workforce had just been warned there would be layoffs. Their biggest customer had recently started buying its titanium slag from a competitor in Canada. Pretty soon Zinken would be the only factory left in Odda working full-time.

I checked my messages. None from Irene. I recalled the bundle of letters in the glove compartment. I hadn't removed them last night. Maybe she'd found them early this morning. That must have been why she had disappeared. She'd found them and wanted to confront my brother with them. I texted her: *Where are you?*

We were through the tunnel. Ask braked by the rubbish tip. It stank. People called that tunnel on the Tyssedal road the Arsehole because it always smells of shit there. On warm days like this the smell was even worse. Ask said they weren't really going any further, but he could drop me off in Odda if I wanted. I said yes. We trundled on towards the centre.

Mumuki likes you, said Ask. Did you know

that? Fine man, she says. Robert is a fine man. Did you get anything that night?

I looked over at Ask.

Do you want her? he asked. You can have her. You're unmarried, unattached. You need some regular pussy, right? You can't go on messing around with Skjeggedal women for the rest of your life. She's yours. I'm ready for something new. A black one maybe.

I remained silent. Ask was the type of man certain women fell for. He had a big mouth. All the same, I felt there was a smaller, gentler man inside the big one.

I'm just mucking you about, you know that? said Ask.

He apologised for what had happened on Monday evening. They'd had too much to drink, and everybody was pissed off about what had happened to the Pedersen kid.

We hummed in towards the centre. The pale morning floated between the buildings. The cars glinted in the sunlight; the day was going to be just as hot as the ones before it. Same old story.

By the way, heard any more about the fire? said Ask.

Fire?

Yeah, at the asylum seekers' hostel.

Ask said it was a nasty piece of work. Something like that really pissed him off.

There weren't many of us in Odda, and we were getting fewer by the day. Those of us still left ought to be able to manage to live in peace. It was the least you could ask. And how difficult could that be?

22

Follow the experts' advice on happiness, it said on the front page of *Dagbladet.* I skimmed quickly through the paper in the shop but found nothing there about the fire. That may only have been because it had happened late last night.

I walked along the harbour promenade towards the floating jetty. The duck was swimming about in the bay with her ducklings in tow. Now there were only three left. Ronaldo was nowhere to be seen. I wondered if I should take a trip up to the hostel. I had a hunch he might be in trouble.

Back at the *BT* office Erik Bodd sat with his feet up on the table. He'd made himself coffee and found a Coke in the fridge. I asked what he was doing in my office.

Your office?

Yes, my office.

So this is your office? I thought it was *BT*'s office. We do work for the same newspaper, don't we?

Bodd said he'd tried to get in touch with me during the night. There had been a fire at the asylum seekers' hostel. We usually covered fires in *Bergens Tidende*. Or perhaps I didn't think there was a story in that either?

I asked about the fire. Bodd said the alarm had gone off in the middle of the night. All the asylum seekers had been safely evacuated. Four Kurds had managed to put it out themselves. It was probably an arson attack. The fire had broken out in two places at once. I was relieved. Ronaldo must be all right. I asked if there were any suspects. Bodd didn't know. All he knew was that the three Serbs hadn't been at the hostel last night. At first the manager thought they might have got trapped inside, but the trio turned up again later.

We were trailing them in the evening, said Bodd. But we lost them.

According to Bodd's sources, the three of them didn't usually spend the night at the hostel. They stayed out at night and slept during the day.

You're a local guy, said Bodd. Where do you think they go?

Haven't a clue, I answered.

Is it drugs? Women? Have they got the local girls after them?

Bodd stood up and put his face close to mine.

They weren't with you, were they? You weren't at home last night either.

I smelt Bodd's odours. Coffee and aftershave. I said I'd been out along the fjord. Been visiting my ex. She had some trouble with flooding in the cellar. Bodd asked if I'd got any — sex with your ex could be heaven or it could be hell.

He asked if I'd seen the papers. He opened *VG*, with a picture of Pedersen posing outside the house at Buer. Beneath an 'Odda killing' vignette the heading was spread across two pages: *My son had no enemies*. Bodd waited for me to say something. I felt inviolable as long as I could still feel Irene's touch. That feeling would last for a few more hours yet. Then it would be submerged by everything that made me a man who could not be trusted.

Bodd said: Talkative bloke. At least, for someone who won't talk to the press.

Some people have to be protected from themselves, I said.

Protected from themselves? said Bodd. What the fuck does that mean? How would you react if someone said that about you? That you had to be protected from yourself?

He turned over several pages and spread two stories out side by side on the table.

See? They've both got dogs . . .

The tabloids had almost identical stories about the dead boy's Alsatian. Even the

140

pictures were almost the same. Bodd laughed and said they must be soft in the head. Interviewing a dog. Making the story about a dog.

He outlined how we should spend the rest of the day. Find out what the detectives and the local lawman were up to. Consider going door to door in the neighbourhood. He'd had the Serbs checked for criminal records, but there was more to go on. Check their identities; maybe they weren't who they said they were.

The office phone rang. Bodd answered. He grinned and looked at me.

Oh yes, he's here now.

He handed me the receiver. I heard the desk editor say she'd had a query from TV2, who were doing a live broadcast from the pedestrian precinct in the evening. They wanted me and my brother, since we knew the case so well and were both in our way investigating it from different angles.

I said I didn't think I fancied it.

She waited for a few moments. She said she expected us to work as a team. I should do it for the paper. It would be a good showcase for the paper. I just wanted to hang up, but she added quickly that there was one other thing. She said I'd probably already noticed that in today's paper there was an invitation for readers to respond to government policy on immigration. People could send e-mails or ring between four and six. Since I knew about this particular case it would be a good thing if I would take the calls.

I didn't say anything.

That's great then, she said.

And there were two other stories she wanted me to work on. She had read a report which said that screen villains made bad role models for young immigrants who felt they weren't doing well. I should have a word with the local video shop about it. And she also wanted me to do something on a background issue which would put the events in a different perspective. It would be good if I could find some former trade union big shot who'd lost his job and now blamed it on the foreigners.

We need a person, she said.

I didn't answer. She said the background story was the priority. We had to show how racism arose, that racism had its causes.

You're right, I said. Racism comes from somewhere.

Then we're agreed on that, she said.

No, I don't think so.

Why not?

It's people like you who create racism, I said. Racism comes from people like you.

142

From people sitting in an office who think they know what this is about.

She was quiet for a few moments. Then she said that she would like to see a scan of the inside of my head, I had so many interesting thoughts. But we'd have to leave that for another day. She said all she did was interpret the available information. She just picked up on trends and currents. That was her job. She analysed and suggested angles of approach. My job was to find the man.

He doesn't exist, I said.

Then make him up.

I hung up and turned to Bodd. I told him to get out of my office. He stared at me and shook his head. Then he picked up his Coke and headed for the door. In the entrance he stopped.

One thing I forgot, he said. I played a few hands on your computer. Lost a couple of hundred dollars. Hope that's okay. You're still up fifty thousand.

23

I missed the rain. Everything being wet. Everything being kissed. Everything being clarified. Rain falling on the streets. Wipers moving back and forth across the windscreen. Bodywork glistening in the street lights. Now I drove round pointlessly. The sunlight blinded me. Everyone around me had disappeared. They were gone, and I didn't know where to look.

The mobile rang as I was on my way home for a shower. The store manager at the supermarket said they'd caught a kid shoplifting. The boy refused to speak to anyone but me. They'd found my card in his pocket. I said I could be there in five minutes. The Fjord Shopping Centre was right next to the floating jetty. It was the kind of shopping centre you found in all Norwegian towns. A place where old people stood glued to the one-armed bandits and little children howled for sweets. A place where people spent all the money they didn't have on things they didn't need.

Ronaldo sat in a side room in his Brazil shirt, with his back to the wall. He didn't look at me when I came in. A security guard with a shaven head said hello. I recognised him. He was one of the Reservists who had attacked me that night. I'd also interviewed the guy when he won the car stereo national championships, a competition to see whose car had the loudest stereo.

Are you responsible for this boy? the skinhead asked.

I didn't answer and turned to the store manager: What has he done?

The store manager said the boy had tried to steal a loaf of bread and a packet of buns.

Why did you do it? I asked Ronaldo.

He stared straight ahead without answering.

Why did you do it? the skinhead repeated and gave Ronaldo a shake.

I took his hand away. I told him to take it easy.

No one tells me to take it easy.

I'm asking you to take it easy, I said.

The skinhead turned to Ronaldo again: Can't you talk? You can shoplift, but you can't talk?

I moved between Ronaldo and the guard.

Are you on drugs? I asked.

The guard stood so close to me I could see the drops of sweat on his scalp.

D'you shave yourself down there as well? I asked.

At first I thought he was going to hit me, but he just stood quite still. Finally Ronaldo looked up. I turned to the store manager and told him I would speak to the boy. The store manager said he would report him to the police if it happened again.

I nodded to the skinhead as we left: Have a nice day.

In the car outside I decided to sit quietly until Ronaldo said something. He had that same sour look on his face and I wondered if I actually liked him or just felt sorry for him. A fat couple wheeling a full trolley emerged from the shopping centre. The woman waddled over towards the car park. The man placed a weary hand over the topmost plastic bags to prevent anything falling out. He looked at me with sad eyes as he passed by. From the outside we probably looked like father and son sitting in the car. It was a normal day. We'd been to the shopping centre. Something or other had happened, and we couldn't find the words to talk about it.

At last I said: Somebody should do something about this heat.

Ronaldo turned towards me.

I just wanted them to have something to eat, he said.

I know.

I started the car. We drove through the

146

centre of town. A cop stood in the square talking to a group of Reservists. His name was Even Storheie. He'd been suspended from his job after the papers revealed how he'd been recruiting people to a pyramid scheme. Now it looked as if his superiors had let him out of the cupboard again on account of the killing.

I drove along the eastern arm of the fjord. I told Ronaldo he would have to stop feeding the ducks. It was the only solution. If he stopped feeding the ducks, the seagulls would probably disappear too.

But they must have food, protested Ronaldo. Without food they'll die.

That's how it is, I said. Trouble every day.

I drove with no clear idea of where I was going. We just drove on beside the fjord. At the bathing beach I pulled over and parked the car. Through the trees I saw there were plenty of people down there. Usually people travelled further out along South Fjord to swim. This beach had been established before the fjord had been pronounced the most polluted in the world. Now it was so hot it looked as though people didn't care a damn what it was they were hopping into.

Ronaldo asked if I was a policeman. I laughed and said I was a journalist.

How old are you? he asked.

Thirty-eight, I answered. You can saw me in half and count the rings.

We walked down the path. I took off my shoes and felt the rocks burning under my feet. It was humid; a few thunderclouds had gathered above the mountains. Over on the south side of the beach a family of Tamils had withdrawn into the shade of the trees where they were preparing food and playing badminton.

Go and have a swim, I said to Ronaldo.

He stood at the water's edge. I thought he looked embarrassed. He didn't want people to see how fat he was. I took off my shirt, thinking it might make it easier for him if he saw I wasn't embarrassed, even though I was a bit chubby myself.

It isn't cold, I said.

He just stood there.

Come on, I said. Have a dip.

The Reservist guy annoyed me. I'd rescued him from the reservist guy in the shop. I'd taken him out here so that he could enjoy himself. Why couldn't he just jump into the fucking water and enjoy himself?

Try and enjoy yourself, I called out. Make an effort.

He looked at me.

That's what people usually do in summer, I said.

I took hold of his top and was going to pull it over his head. He resisted.

Isn't that why you came here? I shouted. To have a bit of fun?

He looked at me. Then he pulled off his top.

I took him by the upper arm and led him out on to the concrete breakwater.

Are you going to dive or jump? I asked.

By now the other bathers had noticed us and were watching with interest.

Are you going to dive or jump? I shouted again.

Ronaldo looked at me.

I can't swim, he said.

I stood there. The sunlight reflecting from the fjord dazzled me. I closed my eyes. For a few moments I just stood there, like someone without a script who doesn't know what's supposed to happen next. I thought that I was nothing, just a fat man on the beach. Then I turned, picked up my shirt and put it on again. Ronaldo came shuffling along behind me. We got into the car and drove back in to Odda.

I don't know why, but halfway there I began to cry. I drove into the sunlight and cried and the landscape beyond the windscreen disappeared.

You've got the wipers on, said Ronaldo.

He was right. I had got the wipers on. I couldn't remember turning them on. We drove into the centre with the wipers swishing across the dry windscreen.

Aren't you going to turn them off? asked Ronaldo.

No.

But it isn't raining.

He was right about that too. It wasn't raining.

24

Ronaldo disappeared across the car park and away up the street. I sat there a bit longer with my hands on the steering wheel. I heard the ticking of the Volvo as the engine gradually cooled. A wind had got up. Several clouds had appeared in the north. They were light on top and dark underneath, as if all the badness in them had congregated in their bellies.

I walked over to the diner. The asphalt was soft beneath my shoes. Inside I caught sight of Tor behind a curtain. He was busy cooking something. I called out a greeting. I ordered a fried egg sandwich and a beer. A copy of *Bergens Tidende* lay on the counter. The entire front page was covered with a picture of the burnt-out BMW. *Car wreck may be key to murder riddle,* said the headline.

Inside the paper it seemed that the police didn't want to say much about the car after all. My piece on the protest march was in as a side-bar. There was an editorial about the murder. Everyone involved had to show restraint and let the police do their job, was the message. It added that we could no longer deny that there were real problems associated with globalisation and immigration. What we were seeing were the outlines of a collision of values.

My mobile rang. A woman from TV2 told me I should be there at seven for make-up and a dry run. Frank and I would be on towards the end of the broadcast. It would be good if I could give some consideration as to how this business might change Odda, and what it was like for me to be covering a story in which my own brother was one of the investigators. Were we competitors, or could we work together?

Tor sat down at the table to keep me company. He dug out a cigarette and nodded towards the paper. He asked if anyone had been arrested. I shook my head. He said murder was good for business. They had a lot of people in last night. They hadn't had such a good night since the fixer for Cohen Brothers came over from the States. He bought drinks for half the town during the months he was here.

Maybe it's a potential growth area for the town? said Tor.

What?

Murder. A murder a week would generate more income than all the retraining plans put together.

And who's going to do the murders?

The mayor, of course.

Tor said he had real faith in murder. It was guaranteed to move Odda up the list of towns that were currently booming. According to a recent report, Odda was now bottom.

I ate quickly and hungrily. I hadn't eaten since yesterday afternoon. I washed the sandwich down with the beer.

Tor said the people who lived in Odda were dying out anyway. But not quickly enough, he added. No one notices when you die that slowly. You have to die a quick and brutal death. Otherwise the press don't come.

He said there was something strange about the press. On their own they seemed like decent people. But as soon as they got in a crowd they changed completely. He'd seen two TV crews in action yesterday. They'd stopped a girl who was cycling over the bridge by the Shell station. She was on her way to the gym and probably had nothing at all to do with the Pedersen kid. But they got her to lay a bouquet of flowers on the bridge. Of course she wasn't carrying any flowers, so they used a bouquet that was already there.

Tor asked if I'd ever considered a change of career. Doing something completely different. Write a book or go travelling. I shrugged.

I'd often thought I should go away and try

something new. Back in my office I'd hung up a photo from *National Geographic*. It was of six American researchers preparing for a voyage to Mars. They went round in spacesuits and lived in isolation outside Hanksville, a small town in southern Utah. I'd had offers of other jobs on the paper. The editor-in-chief had at one time wanted me to take charge of the new City section. But it would have meant moving to Bergen, and I couldn't stand the thought of being so far from Irene. And the union had refused me permission to accept the offer anyway. They thought the editor-in-chief would take the chance to close the local office and give the Odda job to a stringer. I'd explained that the office had already been closed down. I was already walking round wearing a spacesuit somewhere outside Hanksville.

You were always so good at school, said Tor. You were good at all subjects. Kids are usually good at one or two subjects, but you were good at all of them.

I'd eaten too quickly and I felt nausea rise up in me. I went to the toilet to wash my hands. My face in the mirror was white. I looked away and dried myself slowly. I paid and said so long to Tor. He shouted that I should think about what he'd said about murders. I said I'd write a leader about it.

Even as I was letting myself into my office I heard the phone ringing. Inside I picked up the receiver and put it down again. A few seconds later it rang again, as though the phone had only been taking a breather.

Hello, hello! I shouted at the handset.

I was back on Boogie Street.

I'd been doing a regular phone-in column for over a year. The new editor-in-chief wanted to make reader response a growth area. The threshold was to be lowered. Every voice should get a hearing. Ordinary people should have access to the column. The trouble was that the only people who called in were idiots. Every afternoon between four and six it was like opening a sewer. Every joker was more than happy to empty his shit over the telephone and land it right on your desk. In the end I couldn't stand it any more. The column was fobbed off on some other poor jerk.

Now, damnit, if I wasn't dancing down Boogie Street again. The phone went on ringing. There was just a brief pause before it rang again. I didn't answer, just shouted, Hello, hello, you sick bastard, how are we today! I turned the volume down almost to zero and turned on the computer. I played Tripeaks, trying to win back the dollars that prick Erik Bodd had lost.

25

A guy from the desk called me on my mobile. He said they'd had complaints; callers weren't getting through. I explained that I took the calls as quickly as I could. Right now I was having a conversation with a good old-fashioned racist from Byrkjelo. If I was just left to work in peace I'd get all his crap down word for word. I finished the conversation and went back to my game of Tripeaks. The telephone kept ringing.

What day is it today? I sang. What day is it today?

The desk guy called again. He said he'd tried the land line but got no answer. He wasn't even getting the engaged tone either. What was I actually up to? Was I even in my office at all?

I replied that this was crazy racist day. The Pedersen kid had been found belly up and now every racist was on fire. I was drowning in conversations. Every type of racist was calling in. Great and small. Young and old. National Front and skinhead. Reservists and common or garden racists.

The guy asked me to put the stuff into the

reader-response folder as it came in; they wanted to follow this for all it was worth. They were going to publish some of it on the web along with some e-mails and texts. I asked if it might not be a better idea to wait and then pick out the best ones. There were several outstanding analyses to choose from, with one or two in a class of their own entirely. He said he wanted them in the order they came in.

In order then! I said. You shall have them in order!

I took the next call.

An elderly lady from Bergen told me how her house had dropped in value because a family of Kurds had moved into the street. I didn't respond but kept on playing on screen as she spoke. At last she became uncomfortable and asked if I was still there.

Yes, of course, I answered. Your every word is being noted down.

She said Norwegians just wanted to live in peace. Norwegians didn't want rapes and stabbings and drug dealing. Now was the time for those of us who were paying the price to say stop. It was well past time. I asked for her name. I knew from experience that was a good way of shutting people up.

I thought you could be anonymous, she said.

Oh yes, you can be anonymous, but all racists have to give their full name.

She asked if I was calling her a racist.

Well, what do you call yourself? I asked.

The next caller had an Odda accent. He said we had to start speaking out. The Muslims were heading north. They'd already advanced deep into Europe. This was about values. Soon they would be here too.

Europe will end up Islamic if the fundamentalists get what they want, he said.

And what do the fundamentalists want? I asked.

Well, just look right here in Odda. They killed a white man in cold blood.

Who are they?

The Serbs.

So they did it?

Yes, everyone knows that.

And they're Muslims too?

There was silence.

I said: Well, it is my great pleasure to inform you that the Serbs are not Muslims. They are Christians.

Still silence.

Did that upset you? I asked. Did I spoil your day?

It makes no difference what they are, said the guy. They're a danger to democracy and to Christian values.

The Christians, you mean?

No, these asylum seekers.

We are all Serbs, I said, and hung up.

The new editor-in-chief had called the public 'the great detective'. We have to use the public, invite them into the paper, make use of their knowledge. I longed for the great detective to shut up. Or to get out a bit more and find out what was really happening.

In the opinion of the next caller there was now an uncontrolled flood of them crossing the border.

Racists, you mean?

He didn't listen. He gave me a lecture on how we were becoming a major importer of terrorist scum. We feather-bedded killers and rapists. He asked: And what will be left of Norway? And gave the answer himself: Nothing.

Don't you agree? he asked.

I waited before asking him if he really wanted to know what I thought. He said he'd very much like to hear my opinion. I said I would tell him what I thought.

There are no immigrants, I said.

He didn't reply. I repeated what I had said. I asked him to think about it. He could call me back when it dawned on him what I meant.

You're not supposed to have an opinion, said the caller.

It's not an opinion, I said. It's fact. There are no immigrants.

The man ended the conversation. I noted down his number, traced him on the net and wrote a statement in his name. I sent it off with the following summary: *There are no immigrants, is the conclusion reached by Jan Ove Lagreid from Askøy.*

Once again I strolled along Boogie Street. I opened the sewers, I opened my arms to all the crap, I swam in the shit. After two hours I had had about thirty callers. Most of them wanted to remain anonymous. But I found their names on the net and every time wrote down the opposite of what they'd said. Once I had finished the desk guy from Bergen called me. He said he'd read the contributions with a growing surprise. He noted that every contribution ended with the observation that there were no immigrants. Was I deliberately trying to get fired or what?

Hey! I shouted. You should always listen to the great detective.

26

The sky had grown darker. It would rain soon. The world had come to Hanksville, and I didn't know how to handle the situation. There was no standard programme I could connect to, no usual procedure to follow, no manual of instructions to look things up in.

The desk editor rang. She wondered how the phone-in had gone. I said I had thirty great comments lined up. She asked if I could get out on another story, a fat woman stuck in a garden chair in Tyssedal. Apparently the fire brigade was there already and trying to get her out. I asked if I'd heard her correctly: was she calling me out to write about a fat woman stuck in a garden chair?

Yes, she answered, adding that it was possible the woman had been drinking. Perhaps she needed protecting against herself. But it might be an amusing story, and the picture would be fantastic. Now that we had a photographer on the spot. I said I was busy working on the video story. I'd checked which videos were most popular among young immigrants. Right now I was looking through the films I'd borrowed from the local video store.

She asked what the films were.

Hum Tum, I said. And *Tum Hum*. And then there's *Hum Tum Tum*.

Are they violent?

No, but there's a lot of dancing and kissing.

Kissing?

Yes, really heavy petting.

She said: I give up.

She hung up. I carried on playing Tripeaks. My addiction to the game irritated me, yet it was a kind of meditation. You didn't need to think. Your head vanished inside the machine, you were gone.

There was a knock on the door. I called out that it was open. Frank came in. He asked if I was busy. A kind of panic took hold at the back of my head. I couldn't think what he wanted. Frank had never come up to my office before.

Nice office, said Frank.

He didn't mean it. No one could in all seriousness call it a nice office.

We're on TV today, said Frank.

I nodded.

Apparently the whole point is that we're brothers, he said. Is that how journalists think?

I don't know, I'm not a journalist.

Frank smiled. He said he'd considered not doing it, but after discussing it with his colleagues decided in the end to go through with it. We weren't going to talk about the actual case. And, besides, it was better to have people who knew what they were talking about than clowns who just sat there guessing. I poured us some coffee and asked about the investigation. Frank said they'd had a huge response from the public. They'd interviewed over fifty people so far, but still had no critical eyewitness.

He was silent for a moment.

But that's not what I want to talk about, he said.

Here we go, I thought. He knew about us. He'd found out. Of course he knew. He had a nose for stuff like that. He was a cop. I wondered what he knew. I wondered what he knew that I didn't. Not just about Irene, but also about *her*.

You probably know Irene almost better than I do, said Frank.

I said nothing. He was bluffing. Trying to trip me up. He wanted me out in the open. I'd better have a smart answer.

Has something happened? I asked.

Frank said that yesterday evening Irene had gone to see a friend in Rosendal. She was going to stay the night there and be back today. He'd just had a call from the kindergarten. Irene hadn't been to pick up the kids as agreed. Frank called the friend in Rosendal. Irene hadn't been there. They hadn't arranged anything.

I couldn't think straight. Something had happened to Irene. It had already occurred to me that if she was involved in an accident or something happened to her, I wouldn't be the first to know. I was the one who loved her best, but others would find out long before me. The doctors and the police would contact everyone but me.

What d'you think has happened? I asked.

My brother said he had no idea. He wanted to know what I thought. Maybe I knew something he didn't. I knew the people she hung around with, the places she liked to go. All of it might be relevant. I thought he was trying it on again. Trying to trick me. I had to think clearly. I shook my head and said I had to go to the toilet.

I left, sat down on the toilet seat and lit a cigarette. My brother knew about us. He was a cop. He knew about stuff like this. I'd asked Irene about it too. Then it won't be up to us to decide any more, was what she said.

Suddenly I realised what Frank really wanted. He'd turned up at my office with the intention of going through my things. Maybe he'd already been through my stuff at home. Now he was probably taking his chance while I sat here. He'd be disappointed. I'd got rid of every letter, every card, every e-mail.

I stubbed out the cigarette and had a piss. I thought of Irene and last night. My cock stiffened in my hand and I came quickly. I was glad. It made me calmer. I still had the drop on my brother. Afterwards I stared at myself in the mirror. I thought that I wasn't such a bad man. I thought that I wasn't such a good one either.

Frank was sitting in the office chair when I came back into the room, talking into his mobile. His face was turned towards the window. The back of his head was only just visible over the top of the chair. I saw how alike we were. It was as if I were sitting there myself. For once I was able to see myself. I was a man at work. It was just another day at the office. I felt a twinge of sympathy. Not only had I taken his wife from him, I'd deprived him of his honour as well. I thought of all the other people I could have crossed. The idiots I could have chosen for my worst enemy. I had to choose my own brother.

Frank heard me there and swivelled round.

That's okay, I said and sat down in the visitor's chair.

Frank ended the conversation. We sat for a

few moments in silence. The office phone rang. My first thought was that it was Irene trying to get hold of me and tell me what had happened. My brother said I should just go ahead and take the call. I didn't get up. The phone stopped ringing. My mobile started ringing. I sat calmly, didn't take the call. Frank looked at me.

You know me, he said. You know what I'm like.

What d'you mean?

I'm no angel.

Frank waited.

But I love her. I can't lose her. Do you understand?

I nodded.

Frank stood up and asked me to get in touch if I heard anything or thought of anything. He said anyway we'd talk again before the TV broadcast. He had to get back to the office now. Mother had the kids.

I followed him out into the corridor. Then I sat back down in the office chair. A strange calm seeped into me. He didn't know anything. Hadn't a clue. Irene had left him. She'd found the old letters in the glove compartment and made up her mind to leave him. She'd gone missing for a couple of days to do what she had to do. She'd talked about it before. Going away and being on her own.

Now she'd done it. Everything would work out.

I turned off the computer and locked the door. On the way down the stairs a new unease descended on me. Wouldn't she have rung or left a message? Wouldn't she have picked up the kids from the kindergarten? What had really happened?

At the front door I stopped and peered into the light. I remembered I had a strip of photographs of Irene in the top drawer of my desk. I couldn't bring myself to throw them out. Irene looked so good in them. We'd taken them in a booth at the railway station in Lisbon. In one she was serious. In the middle one she was smiling. In the last one she was pulling a face.

I turned and went back up the stairs. I unlocked the door and opened the drawer. The strip of photographs was gone. Frank had found what he had been looking for.

27

The only sounds in the building came from a vacuum cleaner further down the corridor. A faint whistling died out at the same time as the humming of the vacuum cleaner. The room smelt of dust and sweat. I heard cars in the street outside and imagined each one being driven by Irene. Soon she would park down by the church and cross the square. In a minute or two I'd hear her footsteps coming up the stairs and along the corridor. She would knock on the door and come in.

I don't know how long I sat there. Finally I got up and went to the Låtefossen Bar. Not many in. Blondie had wiggled herself up on to a bar stool. Her skirt was much too short, her laugh much too loud. I thought of leaving but ordered a double whisky instead.

Have you gambled away all your savings? asked Blondie.

I asked if I could buy her a drink. We drank to each other.

She looked at me as she drank.

You and me, Robert. Why didn't it happen?

I shrugged.

Know what I think? she said. You know me

too well. You like people because you don't know them. When you get to know someone, you lose interest. If you didn't know me as well as you do, you'd come back home with me.

I didn't know you were a philosopher, I said.

Nor did I, Blondie laughed.

I thought I might as well go home with her. I was finished here. I could sit on that bar stool and get drunk with her. And then go home with her.

Everybody knows everybody in Odda, said Blondie. Things can't work out when everybody knows everybody else.

Maybe we could pretend, I said. You don't know me and I don't know you. We're two complete strangers.

I don't talk to strangers, she said.

I'm not that bad when you get to know me, I said.

Okay. Who are you then?

I'm the invisible man.

Really? The invisible man?

No past. No future.

And how do I chat up the invisible man?

In the old-fashioned way.

My mobile rang. It was TV2. Someone reminding me to be there at seven. I said I was on my way. I ordered another whisky.

169

The bartender put the glass on the counter.

The mobile rang again. I didn't answer.

Trouble in paradise? asked Blondie.

I could feel the alcohol spreading through my body. I should get up and leave. I stayed where I was. The mobile rang. I turned it on to Silent. Blondie said it would pass.

It always does, she said and stroked my cheek.

She asked if I knew what happiness was. I answered no. She said no one knew. It was impossible to explain happiness. The only thing you could explain was unhappiness. Everybody knew what unhappiness was.

Okay, what is it? I asked.

Sitting on this bar stool, she said. Sitting here and being without the one thing you want more than anything in the world.

The clock behind the bartender said quarter past seven. I had my mobile on the counter. The display window lit up at regular intervals. I had a feeling I was sitting in an airport and being paged over the Tannoy. I had to get my plane. Had to Go to Gate. But I just sat there. I wanted to go on sitting there until I saw the plane lift off into the sky.

One of the local drunks came in.

What's the frequency, Kenneth? shouted the drunk.

He asked if I knew what you'd get if you

threw all the asylum seekers out of Norway. The bartender told him to shut it. The drunk leant forward: What's the frequency, Kenneth?

I thought of driving home. Get a beer out the fridge. Turn the box on. Watch the fifty-seven channels. Pretend it was just another day. The bartender turned up the sound on the television. The broadcast opened with the anchorman live from the pedestrian precinct. He welcomed everyone to Odda. There were a lot of curious onlookers in the background. The anchorman had been on a sunbed and was wearing a summer suit. He had a strange sneer, as if he couldn't even manage to take murder seriously.

I've always wondered if that guy wears a wig, said Blondie.

The bartender hushed her.

An aerial shot of Odda was accompanied by piano music. It was strange, seeing Odda from the air. You think you know what your home town looks like, but from the air it's unknown territory. The basic outline is familiar, the rest is confusing. Coming in close there were pictures of the Opo, policemen, journalists, torches, the procession moving down the pedestrian precinct. A reporter said Odda was a peaceful town in romantic Hardanger. But now the whole place was in a state of shock.

What a load of bollocks, said the bartender. Are you in shock, Blondie?

The way the demonstration was filmed it looked as if half the town was taking part. I thought how the world becomes what you see on TV or read in the papers. The picture of the world becomes the world. You can take a little piece of the world and transform it into anything you want.

The room began to sway as the alcohol kicked in. The world went on its way. The plane took off. The train pulled out. People met each other and left each other. A girl waited for a bus. A boy read a postcard. Traffic jammed. A wrecked car was hoisted from the river.

Blondie shrieked.

My brother was on TV. The anchorman asked how people in Odda had reacted to the murder: had the sense of security gone?

What an idiotic question, said the bartender.

Frank was getting stout, but he carried it well. He said nothing. Absolutely nothing. And the mayor had been roped into it. Elvestad sat there in the pedestrian precinct and talked about how the murder had shocked him, and how his thoughts were with the family and friends. The mayor appeared to have dyed his hair since I spoke to him yesterday. Now it was completely grey.

The anchorman asked: How can Oddudlians re-establish a safe, happy community here?

Oddudlians? shouted the bartender. Odd-ites, you clown!

I'm certain he's wearing a wig, said Blondie.

The drunk told me my mobile was ringing. He said he could tell from the flashing.

You've got good eyesight, I said.

You must take it, said the drunk.

I said I mustn't. I wasn't here. I was the invisible man.

The drunk took the call for me: What's the frequency, Kenneth?

He handed the phone to me. It was the desk editor. She asked if I was okay. I said I was a little busy right now. She asked where I was. I said I'd fallen into the river and was struggling to reach the bank. Could she ring me later?

There was silence. The drunk sniggered. The desk editor said I should take a couple of days off. Unwind. Maybe get away some-where. It would do me good.

Look after yourself, said the desk editor.

I said that luckily I had a large log to hold on to, but I was afraid I might soon get cramp in the cold water.

Call if there's anything we can do, she said.

The drunk asked for the phone. He said hello and asked if he could tell a joke: What do you get if you throw all the asylum seekers out of Norway?

The desk editor had hung up.

What's the frequency, Kenneth? the drunk shouted.

The broadcast was over. The bartender zapped through the channels and stopped at the highlights from the Brazil — Costa Rica game. The Brazilians were terrific and beginning to look like clear favourites. I don't know whether it was the alcohol or the Brazilians' yellow shirts, but something clicked inside my head. Something opened up. Something slotted into place. I knew I had to get up and get out into the light. I couldn't go on sitting there. I knew I had to stand up and get my suit crumpled, like a journalist.

I asked for the bill.

Are you leaving? asked Blondie.

I have to powder my nose, I said.

Stop playing around, said Blondie.

One hour more light, said the drunk.

As I was paying, something slipped out of my wallet. It was the pictures of Irene. They'd been in my wallet the whole time. I picked up the strip and looked at Irene. She looked so lovely in those pictures.

28

Thunder rolled over the mountains and the clouds looked full to bursting, but the rain didn't come. I got into the Volvo and drove round the centre of town. I coasted up by the floating jetty, along Skulegata, round the town hall, in and out of side streets, past the pedestrian precinct where the TV crews were packing up their gear after the broadcast.

No yellow jersey.

There weren't many people about. Maybe they were waiting for rain. I drove up to the asylum seekers' hostel and parked by the lake. For some reason or other I'd imagined there would be security guards or policemen standing outside, but you could just walk right in. In reception I could still smell burning.

A black man was washing up in the kitchen. He greeted me then turned back to the washing up. I walked into the day room. People sat around in small groups. Some were smoking, some watching TV. A baby was asleep in its mother's lap. The rest sat and vegetated. The clock on the wall said eight thirty.

I coughed and said I was looking for a boy. I realised I didn't know his name.

Ronaldo? I tried.

People smiled or looked down.

Ronaldo? I tried again.

I got no answer. The room was quiet. The clock ticked. I felt a hand on my shoulder. I turned to see a thin, bearded man. He told me to follow him. I did as he said. We went down the corridor to a door with a name plate: *Folkedal*.

The person I took to be Folkedal sat behind a writing desk, picked up a pen and fidgeted with it. He had to be new, I'd never seen the guy before. Folkedal stared at me as if I was a lousy weather forecast.

Might I ask what you're doing here? he said.

I answered that I was looking for a boy who lived at the hostel. Folkedal wanted to know his name. I said he was nine years old and went around in a Brazil shirt. Folkedal waited. Then he asked if I wanted to hear what he'd like to do to all the journalists who had turned up at the hostel over the last few days.

I'm not here as a journalist, I said.

I know who you are.

Okay. Then I won't waste time introducing myself.

I didn't say anything else. When strangers

asked me what I did, I usually replied that I worked on a newspaper. Then it wasn't necessarily a hundred per cent certain I was an idiot. I might be a typographer, or a secretary, or a driver, or the bloke that changes the light bulbs.

Folkedal said: Journalists talk about social responsibility and freedom of expression. They always think they're doing an important job, but in the end it's just about throwing a few stories together, isn't it? Knocking up some story. Sticking a few odds and ends together and making a story.

I didn't protest. I understood something I should have understood before. Ronaldo had talked about being out late, about getting ticked off, about the dead man he'd seen. Dean Martini had talked about the river that became a floating bear. Little boys who should beware of the river. I should have read the signs a long time ago.

Folkedal sat on his desk.

Have you been drinking? he asked. You smell of alcohol.

I like to keep my bodily fluids in balance, I said.

In balance?

Yes. It's something I've learnt to do.

He waited. Then he said he wanted to tell me a story.

Imagine a boy who's been taken to a foreign country, said Folkedal. Maybe he's with his uncle. Maybe some other relative. Maybe at the airport the boy is told to wait by a public telephone. The uncle says he needs to borrow the boy's passport. He says the boy has to wait there until the phone rings. He has to promise not to move until the phone has rung. In the evening, when the airport is closing down, the security guards find a boy standing by a public phone. A boy waiting for a call that never comes.

Folkedal walked over to the window before sitting down again.

Wasn't that a good story? he asked. Do you want to hear some more?

I looked down.

Folkedal said: Have you heard the one about the bloke who was tricked on board a ship he thought was going to Italy? On board he was asked if he would sell one of his kidneys. If he refused, they'd throw him overboard. For the money he'd get for his kidney he could buy a cow, a washing machine, and a plane trip for his kids.

I asked where the boy was from.

He's from Romania, said Folkedal. He's from Albania, from Moldova, from Hungary. Who knows?

What's his name?

It's Stefan. It's Thomas. It's George. Who knows?

Is he here now?

Who knows? He could be anywhere.

Folkedal took out a pack of cigarettes and lit up without offering me one.

He's a gypsy, you do know that?

Folkedal said this as if it explained everything.

I said nothing.

I was looking for him just now but couldn't find him. What do you want with him? Is it about the murder?

Folkedal had talked his way out of his anger and was now willing to listen to me. But I didn't know quite what to say. All I knew was that I had an uneasy feeling about Ronaldo. I gave Folkedal my card and asked him to ring if the boy showed up.

No harm in dreaming, said Folkedal.

I thanked him and left the office. I stuck my head into the day room where everyone had been sitting about a quarter of an hour earlier. Only the hands on the clock had moved. Instead of heading for the exit I climbed the stairs to the first floor. People sat out in the corridor and inside their rooms. They stared at me with a mixture of scepticism and disquiet. In one room three men each sat at different computers. One wore an Eminem vest. Two of them were searching a site called *findafriend* or something like that.

I went out to the Volvo and drove over to Eidesmoen. It struck me that the asylum seekers didn't belong here. They didn't belong here and they did everything they could to try to belong. I thought it was tough enough for those who did belong here.

Up on Erraflot the houses clung to the mountainside. I parked in my usual place. I caught glimpses of the kids inside. The TV was on. A veil of rain approached down the valley. The shower was stretched like a wet curtain between the mountains. The heat of the last few days exploded in enormous drops of rain. In a moment everything was soaked. Frank came racing out into the garden to rescue newspapers, pillows, clothes. I sank down behind the steering wheel, but he was too busy to notice me.

I had stood here so many times. At one time I parked outside the house every evening. I sat and smoked and hoped I might see Irene in there. Occasionally she came out, and we would exchange a few words. She hated me standing outside like that.

She was the only one I absolutely must not love. Perhaps that was why I loved her. Perhaps I couldn't love what I owned.

Perhaps I could only love what was not mine. I didn't know. At some point I had simply come to the conclusion that I loved her.

It was strange. I had waited out here so long. I had wanted her to be mine. Now all I wanted was for her to be in there with her family. Cuddle her children and read to them before they fell asleep.

The rain beat down on the windscreen, the pavement, the rooftops. I dialled her home number. Frank took the call immediately. I asked if there was any news. He said no. He was partly visible in the window, but I couldn't see his face.

Why didn't you turn up for the broadcast? asked Frank.

I didn't answer. He asked again.

I'll tell you some other time, I said.

You might as well tell me now.

We were both silent for a few moments. I played with the steering wheel, the radio dial.

Where are you? he asked.

I just got home, I said.

Silence again.

Have you been drinking?

Only a couple.

And driving?

Only a couple of kilometres.

You're impossible.

Again there was silence for a few moments.

Frank, I want her to come home again, I said.

What do you mean by that? he asked.

What I say.

But why do you put it like that?

I don't know.

I asked if he had thought of reporting Irene as a Missing Person.

I want to have a look myself first, Frank answered.

Where are you going to look?

We'll see.

She can't just vanish into thin air, Frank.

It's happened before. It happens all the time. People just disappear.

She'll be back, I said.

I ended the conversation and sat there with the palms of my hands on my knees. The rain had eased off. The drops had got smaller. I got out and stood beside the Volvo. The rain soaked me, ran over my forehead, throat, chest. I stood there until I was sodden. Then I drove slowly into the centre of town.

29

I found him out by the floating jetty. He sat alone beside a pile of stones. The Brazil shirt was wet and dirty. I sat down beside him. We didn't say anything. The rain had cleared, the clouds driven out along the fjord.

You're fat too, said Ronaldo without looking at me.

I never said you were fat.

But you thought it.

So now you're a mind reader?

He chucked a stone into the water and turned towards me. He saw my soaking wet suit and the hair plastered flat against my head. He smiled. It was the first time I had seen him smile. I asked if he was hungry. He nodded. We got into the Volvo and drove to McDonald's.

After we'd got something to eat I parked on the docks with a view of the town centre and the new promenade. The houses glistened with rain. A sheen of water lay on the asphalt. Ronaldo ate hungrily. I lit a cigarette and wondered why he was fat. He shouldn't be fat. The world was topsy-turvy. Nothing made sense. Suddenly the poor were as fat as the rich. I thought of what Folkedal had told me. Maybe Ronaldo was meant to be the one who made it. The only one who survived to grow up.

He swilled down some Coke and said: When I close my eyes, I see my dad.

You do?

Yes, that's how I think. All I have to do is close my eyes and I can see my dad.

What's your dad like?

Ronaldo smacked his lips and swallowed and didn't say anything.

Can't you remember? I asked.

No.

Then close your eyes and you'll see him.

Ronaldo did as I told him.

What's he like?

He's got black hair. And he's thin.

Like me, eh?

He opened his eyes. We laughed.

I waited a while before asking him if he'd been down by the river that evening the car went off the bridge. He nodded. I asked what kind of car it was. He replied that it was an Opel Ascona.

Not that car, I said. The car behind.

He didn't answer.

Wasn't there another car behind? I asked.

Oh yeah.

Then what kind was it?

A white Subaru Impreza.

What did you say?

A white Subaru Impreza.

How do you know?

Because I was there.

He seemed very sure. He'd answered without hesitation. I was surprised at how much he knew about cars.

What kind of car is this?

A Volvo 240, he answered.

The reply was immediate. I pointed to a car parked over by the quayside.

Mazda 323, said Ronaldo.

He knew them all. He'd been down by the river that night. He'd seen the Opel forced into the river. It was by no means certain it was the Serbs who'd been following the Pedersen kid that night. The BMW definitely wasn't involved. It had been a white Subaru.

Did you see who was driving the Subaru?

He shook his head.

No one got out of the car?

No. The car just drove on.

Will you tell the police this tomorrow?

He looked at me. I realised he was afraid. I wondered if someone had threatened him. Was that why they'd set fire to the hostel? To scare the only witness?

Ronaldo asked if he could have another Coke. I drove off and we bought another large Coke. I stepped outside the car to make a call. Folkedal answered at once. I said I'd found the lad. He was with me now and could stay the night at my place. There was a silence at the other end. Folkedal said he'd been in touch with he paper and heard that I'd been put on sick leave.

What are you up to? asked Folkedal.

You're just going to have to trust me here, I said. The boy is safest with me.

Folkedal said he didn't like it at all, but he didn't know how to stop me. He was at least grateful that I'd let him know. Over in the car Ronaldo had finished eating. He swigged down the last of his Coke and said that now there were only two ducklings left. He didn't know what to do.

Somebody has to keep watch at night, I said.

I waited a few moments. Then I told him he could stay the night at my place. We could discuss what to do about the ducks. He nodded. We drove through the centre. As we drove up the hill at Tokheim a flock of seagulls rose from a garden. They flew in formation over the car and down towards the fjord. One plump gull remained behind, as though too fat to join the others. It settled on top of one of the street lamps.

Back home I changed clothes and asked

Ronaldo if he wanted a shower. He pointed to a picture in the room.

Is that you? he asked.

It was a photo of the Odda team that reached the quarterfinals of the Cup. My father was seated on the right. In another picture my father was standing in front of one of the ovens at the foundry. He was wearing a flat hat and a jacket with the collar turned up. I saw the power that was in him then. It was almost as if more power had been forced into him than his body could take.

No, I said. That's not me.

I made up the bed and sat with Ronaldo until he slept. A spasm went through his body as his muscles relaxed. I stood up and stroked his hair. The Brazil shirt was on the floor. I took it down into the basement and put it into the washing machine. Then I went upstairs again and poured myself a drink. I flipped channels until I found a detective show. A guy in a suit was running down the street with a bandage that covered most of his face.

I thought of how in detective films everything begins in darkness. With each succeeding scene people and events slowly emerge into the light. The past becomes clearer and easier to understand. In the end everything can be explained and the reckoning paid. In reality things happen the other way round. Things seem clear and comprehensible, before they descend into the murk and the muck. As the end approaches you lose all track of the plot and have no idea how it's going to end.

On the teletext I read that three men had been arrested on suspicion of the murder of Guttorm Pedersen. I watched the late news at eleven. There was an interview with the detective guy. He said that three men had been arrested, foreign nationals, and would be charged with murder. There was a live report. The journalist interviewed the detective again and the parish priest, who urged everybody to extend the hand of friendship and stay calm. He asked the press to leave. What Odda needed now was peace and quiet. I closed my eyes. I had thought the world was out of joint. Soon everything would be in place again. I turned off the TV, but kept my finger on the remote. As if I needed some connection with everything that was outside me.

I went down into the basement and hung the Brazil shirt up to dry. Ronaldo slept peacefully up in his room. I heard his breathing and the beating of my own heart. In response to some curious sounds I walked over to the window. A garden sprinkler had got twisted and now wriggled like a snake in

188

the grass. Mumuki appeared. She was wearing white and her black hair hung loose. A half-hearted June moon rolled over Rossnos. Everything lay bathed in a strange light. Streets, houses, cars, telephone wires, clothes lines, Mumuki. She crossed over to the sprinkler. After she had righted the sprinkler she stood in the spray. Slowly, she began to dance on the wet grass.

30

I had fallen asleep on the sofa when the telephone rang at about midnight. Half-asleep I picked up the receiver and said hello. I heard what sounded like breathing at the other end.

Hello? I said again.

No one answered.

I waited, wondering if it was Irene. I wanted to ask her what had happened. I wanted to say I loved her, but I didn't. I couldn't be sure it was her. It could just as well be the guy who had called me up yesterday evening.

Through the receiver I heard a voice, distant and metallic, as if from a loudspeaker at a railway station. I thought it must be someone ringing from far, far away. I remembered what Irene had said about travelling, that if she went away she'd have to take me with her.

The person at the other end sighed.

Then the line went dead.

I stood up and pressed the receiver against my ear, as though the conversation could be prolonged in this way. I found my mobile and rang her number. All I got was a message that the subscriber had turned off the phone or was in an area with no signal. The calm I had just been feeling was suddenly gone. It hit me that out there was a world over which I had no control.

I went into the bedroom to check on Ronaldo. He'd kicked the duvet off but was sleeping comfortably. I covered him again then left the house. The earlier rain had been replaced by a high, clear nightsky. I got into the car and drove into town. Two souped-up cars passed on their way out to the fjord. They were probably going to race in the new tunnel. It was perfect for night driving. No traffic. No speed cameras. No bends. Just a straight road all the way from Odda to Kvinnherad. The politicians talked about the solution to the area's problems being roads, tunnels and bridges. I didn't buy it. All new roads did was give people the chance to get away from here more quickly than ever.

In town a police car drove down Røldalsvegen. I tried to see if my brother was at the wheel, but the car suddenly accelerated and was gone. Apart from that it was quiet in among the buildings, as though the town had died down with the daylight. I wondered who had sent me that video, and why. Somebody was trying to use me for one reason or another. Somebody wanted me to

191

find stuff out. I just didn't know what.

I stopped outside Chinatown. It was closed, and there was light shining from a couple of red lamps. An Asian-looking man was washing down the counter and the floor. I sat in the car and thought how the foreigners came here to do all the shit jobs for us. They wiped our arses for us and tossed us off. And still they got the blame for everything that went wrong.

I drove on and parked at the factory gates by the foundry. I had no idea how I was going to get over or through the barbed wire. My father was sure to know where to find the various holes in the fencing, but it was too late to ring him now. I got out and walked along the fence in a southerly direction.

Passing the fire station I heard a scraping sound behind me. I turned and got a flashlight beam straight in the eyes. Instinctively I put my hands above my head. I could just about see a guard on the other side of the fence. For a moment I thought it must be the skinhead I'd had the exchange with down at the Fjord Shopping Centre.

What are you doing here? asked the guard.

From the voice I realised it was someone else. He continued to hold his torch on me. I put my hands down and wondered what to say.

I'm looking for my cat, I said.

Your cat?

Yes. Jerry.

Jerry?

My cat's name.

Jerry isn't here. You go home now.

The guard waited. I raised a hand and then turned to head back along the fence.

Hey! the guard shouted to me. You don't mean Tom, do you?

Tom?

Yes. Jerry is the mouse.

Oh really?

Tom is the cat, Jerry is the mouse.

I see. I'll check with Jerry when I get home, I promise.

I walked calmly back to the Volvo. I couldn't see the guard, but I felt sure he was watching me from the other side of the fence. The summer moon had disappeared behind some clouds. Somewhere a dog barked. I got into the car and drove back down Røldalsvegen. On the bridge by the Shell station several candles were still burning in memory of the Pedersen kid.

Without thinking I carried on along the east side of the fjord. At the crossroads after the Tyssedal tunnel I turned right and pushed the car up the curves towards Skjeggedal. The headlights swept across the mountainside and the pines. The sense of physical excitement from the previous evening returned now in milder form. Tension in the body. The disquiet as I had driven here with Irene.

By the cabin all was quiet and starry. A couple of lights twinkled on the far side of the water. Voices floated down from the other side of the valley. Some drunken nonsense punctuated by laughter. I leaned on the bonnet and smoked. A little of the heat of the day still lingered between the mountains, but most of it had fallen back into the fjord by now.

I saw myself inside the cabin with Irene, standing behind her and looking up at the stars. I regretted not having said anything when the phone rang. It might have been her. It must have been her. I wanted to get inside the cabin to see if there was anything I had overlooked in the morning. If I didn't find her or she didn't get in touch with anyone, she would be reported missing. They would write about it in the papers. They would call it the *Irene case*. People would be called in for questioning. They'd be out there with dogs, they would be going door to door.

Inside the cabin I looked for the light switch but couldn't find it. I stood a moment in the dark before heading for the room. A sound made me stop. I thought I heard breathing. Maybe I'd forgotten to close the door earlier today and some animal had got in. I stood quite still and wondered what kind of animal it might be. It occurred to me that an animal wouldn't react in this way. Wouldn't it run, or attack?

I entered the room carefully. A voice told me to stay where I was. In the half-dark I couldn't see him all that clearly, but my brother was sitting on the sofa and pointing a rifle at me.

You've always thought you were the smarter of us two, haven't you? said Frank.

31

My brain began working on different explanations, but I was tired of lying. Frank was wearing his uniform with the short-sleeved shirt. I couldn't see his eyes or the expression on his face. I saw only that he was wary of me.

Put down the rifle, I told him.

He didn't do as I told him.

I knew you'd come back, said Frank. You've always been the sentimental type.

Everything comes back, I said. Like a recorded delivery.

What do you mean by that?

I don't know.

Then why did you say it?

It's from a poem.

See? You've always got to be so clever.

I sat down in a chair. I was feeling very cold. My head had been blown empty.

Why are you pointing that rifle at me? I asked.

Why not? replied Frank.

It doesn't feel very comfortable.

Lots of things don't feel very comfortable.

Put the rifle down and let's talk.

We can talk anyway. After all, we're brothers. You talk first. I'm sure there's a lot you want to get off your chest.

Put down the rifle, I said.

I feel safer with the rifle, he said. When I saw the car coming up the valley I thought it was best to arm myself. You never know who's going to pop up. Friend or foe.

He waited for me to say something. I didn't say anything.

What d'you think? said Frank.

About what? I said.

Friend or foe?

I thought that now a different person was sitting on the sofa. He'd become someone else to me, just as I'd become someone else to him. Something had come between us, something that would keep us apart for ever.

Where's your car? I asked.

Frank didn't reply. He waited.

Then he said: She's lying up in the reservoir, isn't she?

Be serious, Frank.

You killed her and dumped her body up there.

No, I did not.

She wouldn't have you, so you killed her. Isn't that what happened?

That isn't what happened.

I ought to shoot you and dump you in the

dam. Then you'd end up in the same place as her. You'd like that, wouldn't you?

Frank stopped. I felt my hand throbbing again.

One thing I don't understand, said Frank. Out of three billion women, why did you have to pick her?

I looked up.

That's not the way it works, I said.

Then how does it work? asked Frank.

I don't know.

You know perfectly well how it works. You know all about how it works.

Suddenly you just can't choose, Frank. Suddenly it's impossible to choose.

Bullshit. You're so full of bullshit I ought to shoot you just because of all the crap you talk.

He got up and approached me. He stood beside the chair and pressed the rifle against my neck. I looked up and thought that he was afraid. As though he was scared of crossing a line and losing his self-control.

Tell me about Irene, said Frank.

Let's stop this now, I said.

Frank pressed the rifle even harder into my neck. I could feel his breath against my cheek.

What was it like being inside her? he whispered.

I don't know.

Did it feel good being inside her? Did you like it?

I don't know.

She's gorgeous, isn't she?

I sat quite still. It seemed to me he was waiting for me to do something, resist, or make some sudden move, so that he could blow my head off.

Sit down Frank, please, just sit down.

For some reason or other he did as I said. He lifted the rifle away, crossed to the sofa and put the weapon on the table. He picked up a bottle of water and drank. I asked for a smoke. Frank took out a pack and a lighter. We smoked for a while without speaking.

I wondered how he had found out. How long he'd known. What he knew. Why he hadn't said anything. Pictures developed on my retina, one image dissolving before the next appeared. A silent slide show. Frank and me. Irene and Frank. Me and Irene.

Have you noticed how fat I am? Frank grinned.

He took hold of his stomach and squeezed his spare tyre.

I'm nearly as fucking fat as you are, he said. A real fat boy.

He took a swig of water. I waited.

He asked: When did it all really start?

I don't know, I answered.

You know. When did it start?

In Lisbon.

You're joking, When did it start?

In Italy. When we were all on holiday in Trieste.

When, Robert?

That New Year's Eve.

When?

The same evening you two became a couple.

Frank shook his head.

I've thought about that so many times, he said. I couldn't believe she would have me. I couldn't believe she was mine. That I could be so lucky.

You've always been the lucky type, Frank.

Yeah. Just look at me now.

He lit another cigarette and handed me the rifle.

He said: Let somebody else kill you, Robert. I'd rather not think about you any more. I've thought about you enough.

I hesitated. Finally I reached out and took the rifle.

Have it, said Frank. I don't need to shoot you. You're already dead.

He sat down again. He said that now I could shoot him. I would be doing him a favour if I shot him. Wasn't that what I'd wanted all along? To get rid of him?

I said nothing.

I'm not kidding, said Frank. You'd really be doing me a favour if you shot me. Is that too much to ask of your own brother?

Shut up, Frank! I said. I pointed the rifle at him.

32

Frank drank some more water. He stared at me as if he was trying to get me into focus. My throat felt dry.

Tell me about Irene, I said.

He said nothing.

Tell me about Irene, I said again.

Frank took another drink.

When did you realise? I asked.

I don't know, he answered.

You know, Frank. When did you realise?

A long time ago.

When, Frank?

1814.

I was standing now. Frank looked up at me. He looked small, sitting there on the sofa. I felt the world twisting round in my head.

She was everything to me, said Frank.

Shut up, I said.

She was, said Frank. She was everything to me.

His whimpering irritated me. My grip on the rifle tightened. I walked towards the sofa.

Tell me, I said.

Tell you what?

Talk.

What d'you want to know?

I want to know what it was like.

What?

Being with her when you knew that I'd had her too.

What's wrong with you, Robert? What the fuck is wrong with your head?

I could see Frank's pale face, but I couldn't see his eyes. I waited.

There's something I want to say to you, I said.

Yeah? said Frank.

We aren't perfect, I said. That's what's so good about people. That's what's so terrible. These things can happen. They happen.

Frank gave a low whistle.

That isn't blood running in your veins, Robert. It's piss.

Shut up, I said.

I pressed the rifle against his neck. My body felt light and heavy at the same time.

Come on, said Frank. Shoot me.

He sat quietly on the sofa. I thought how I could do what he'd said he was going to do. Shoot him and dump his body in the reservoir. I had my finger on the trigger. The room around me disappeared. I could feel my head was almost gone.

Shoot, said Frank.

Now I knew that I was a man who could

make a mistake. I was someone who couldn't be trusted.

Shoot me, said Frank. Stop being a coward. You've been a coward long enough.

I don't know how long I stood there like that. I went on standing there until I could hear the sound of a car engine. Lights shone in through the cabin window. A car drove up the valley and stopped outside. I lowered the rifle.

Too much of a coward even there, said Frank.

We heard footsteps approaching. Someone whistling. Someone knocking. A man in uniform came in. It was Andersen, one of Frank's colleagues. The guy looked at us in confusion, first Frank, then me.

I turned and left without anything else being said. At the car I realised I was still holding the rifle in my hand. I opened the boot and tossed it inside. Inside the Volvo it was cooler. I turned the car round back the way I had come.

When I reached the centre it was almost two. There was no one about. Electric light dribbled out of stores and petrol stations. I wanted a drink, but everywhere was closed. The doors and the shop fronts were just waiting for another day. There was an emptiness about Odda now, something that hadn't been there before, as though the silence of the shutdown foundry had spread out across the whole town.

Driving through the west end the Volvo hummed from one streetlight to the next, caught in the light then disappearing again, caught again in a slow rhythm that made me sleepy. A car appeared behind my Volvo. I slowed down. The car behind did the same. I signalled for him to pass but the car stayed on my tail. On the stretch before Askane I braked hard. The other driver did the same.

I didn't turn up towards Tokheim but carried on along the main road. I considered heading down into the industrial estate at Eitrheim. That was about the stupidest thing I could do. I'd be trapped down there. I put my foot down before entering the tunnel and was doing over a hundred before I got there. The car behind had no difficulty in keeping up.

Leaving the tunnel I slowed down. The car kept close on my heels. In the rear-view mirror all I could see were the headlights. I wondered if it might be an old Volvo. Not until we reached Digranes did he pull out alongside me. A man waved. For a few hundred metres he drove along parallel with me. Then he put his foot down and shot away. I tried to memorise his registration number. His rear lights disappeared round a corner.

I pulled over to the side, turned off the engine and sat there breathing heavily. I'd no idea who the guy was. He looked quite ordinary. He could have been anybody.

33

I dreamt about Frank. We must have collided. He had a cut on his face and blood on his white shirt. We sat in the PV and waited for an ambulance. Frank asked for a smoke. I lit up for him and held the cigarette while he inhaled. He closed his eyes and exhaled. I sat with my arm around him as though we were a pair of lovers out driving.

I woke on the sofa fully clothed. It was past ten. The sounds from outside seemed muted, as though they were held down. A sense of unease brought me to my feet. I checked the phone. Irene hadn't called. I tried to visualise her as I showered. I couldn't do it; all I could see was her pussy and her breasts.

I shaved. The blade made my face tender. I wrote *Irene* in the condensation on the mirror. I thought of how we try to hide what we are. We try, but everything we do shows on our faces. I could see Irene in my face. The lovely places were where she had left her mark. If she were to disappear, the lovely places would disappear from my face too.

Ronaldo was asleep when I took in his breakfast. I shook him until he woke up.

Ronaldo smiled at me. I said I had to call in at work. He could watch the cartoons while I was away. I could turn on the TV and leave the remote on the table.

I want you to stay here, said Ronaldo.

I'll be back soon.

I want you to stay here.

I put the freshly washed Brazil shirt on the bed.

I said: When I get back, we can go to the baths. Would you like that?

He didn't answer.

I can teach you to swim.

He looked up at me.

You're kind, he said.

I stroked his hair.

Not always, I said.

Outside the air was still. The rain had made no difference. Today was going to be just as hot as all the other days. It seemed the whole of the west of the country was having a heat wave.

As I drove into Odda I thought about the time my father had taught me to swim. He showed me the drawings that hung on the wall at the public baths, then he sat by the pool smoking and calling out to me to do like the man in the drawings. I remember the water closing around me. I swam like a dog.

At the office I opened the window before I

started ringing round. I should have thought of it before, I should have realised, but half an hour later I had confirmation of the fact that two cars had been stolen that night. The first was the Serbs' BMW, which Bodd had found at Eitrheim. The other was a Subaru which had been reported stolen on Monday morning. The police had posted details in the usual way. The Subaru still hadn't turned up. The owner was Samson Nilsen.

I searched my pockets for a cigarette but didn't find one. I sat there, trying to see a pattern in what I had discovered. I wanted to know how certain events connected up with others, and what happened as a result of these other events. How was Samson Nilsen involved? Was he the one who'd forced the boy into the river? What had happened to Irene? Were the two things connected? If I found out what had happened to the boy, would I find out what had happened to Irene? All I wanted was for Irene to come back.

I bought cigarettes at the sweet shop and flicked through the papers. Both *VG* and *BT* had identified the Serbs. The picture Martinsen had taken through the window of my Volvo was all over the front page. *Dagbladet* had used silhouette drawings with a few details on each of the accused. The strange thing was that the silhouettes made a more powerful impact than the photographs. The silhouettes made the Serbs look like criminals. The guilty men had been found. The case was solved.

The shopowner came over and stood beside me. He was an irritable little Vietnamese named Nam. People in Odda just called him Viet Nam Nam.

You can't stand here read papers, said Nam.

I looked at him. The guy was quivering with rage.

So I can't stand here and read the papers?

No, roppery.

Roppery?

Yes, roppery. These my papers.

Right. So the papers are yours?

You can't stand here and read papers without money.

Sorry, I didn't know the papers were yours.

If you want read papers, you pay money for papers.

I put *VG* back in the rack and waved goodbye.

Take a course in Norwegian! I said.

Go a libray! Nam shouted after me.

I went back to the Volvo and drove up to Hovden. I parked in the drive of the Bruce villa.

The place was partially shaded by tall fir

trees. A tricycle and a dark green Audi were parked outside the garage. A dog came bounding round the corner. It sneaked out on to the tennis court, squatted and did its business by the net.

The politicians had wanted to pull down the old director's house and replace it with homes for the elderly. To the Labour Party it remained a symbol of the time the managing director Bruce used to more or less run the whole town. But then Samson Nilsen had bought the villa and completely renovated it. I'd heard rumours. At regular intervals Nilsen invited the Odda big shots home to huge parties. He owned three or four cars. He wore expensive suits. People said he had a yacht in Florida and a mistress in Nice. There was talk of exclusive nightclubs and Formula One racing in Monaco. People wondered where the man got his money from. The local rumour-mongering wasn't helped much by reports in the local paper that Samson Nilsen had been given a government grant to run two internet cafés that turned out to be recruitment centres for a pyramid operation. But then people didn't know how big speedway was on the Continent. Samson Nilsen must have been a zloty millionaire many times over.

Sunlight made the view through the

windscreen look faded. I felt hot and nauseous. I didn't know what I was doing there. I was a man in a car outside a house. If someone approached down the driveway and asked what I was doing, I wouldn't know how to answer. That's the way it was. People in the wrong place at the wrong time. If you took a satellite picture of the whole world and managed to identify all the people on it, a surprising number of them would be in the wrong place. My brother once told a story about a firm that specialised in aerial photography. On fine summer days they flew over town and countryside. A few weeks later the salesmen went round offering pictures taken so close up that people were able to recognise their own houses. A young wife down the fjord bought a picture of the family home and had it framed. Her husband, who worked in the North Sea, came home and had a good look at the photo. He fetched a magnifying glass and discovered a car parked there that shouldn't have been there. On the day the picture had been taken his wife's lover had parked his car outside and was inside screwing her.

Around eleven thirty Samson Nilsen came out of the Bruce villa. He was wearing a white shirt and light-coloured trousers. Every time I saw him I had the feeling that here was a guy who could dress up all he liked, but sooner or later you'd notice the specks of oil on his fists. Samson Nilsen pushed his sunglasses up on to his forehead and fished out his mobile phone. He tapped out a text before getting into his Audi.

I stayed on his tail to Eide and then on towards the centre. Nilsen parked outside the Co-op Megastore and went into the bank. Five minutes later he came out again and crossed the road. He bought an ice cream. He met someone he knew. He picked up the day's papers. A veil of air lay between the people and the street, between him and me, between the observed and the observer. The heat created a distance that made me feel easier. I could follow him without being detected. All the same I felt as though I were stealing something from Samson Nilsen. Simple, everyday actions acquired a different quality merely because I was tailing him.

As I followed him I was thinking, this is something you do in other cities. You tail people in Los Angeles, London, Tokyo. Not in Odda. But on a radio programme they'd said it was the easiest thing in the world to tail someone. It doesn't occur to them. No one supposes they might be under surveillance.

34

The oil warning light was on. It had to be a fault with the light itself; I'd just had the car in for a service. We drove south along Sandvin lake. Samson Nilsen drove so fast I was afraid of losing him. Not far from Saga we got stuck in a traffic jam and I was able to ease down. All the same I had no idea how long I intended to follow him.

As we drove I turned on the radio. The announcer said that a demonstration against racism would be arranged this evening. Moreover, *Look and See* magazine had started a memorial fund for Guttorm Pedersen. An editor would be coming to Odda later in the day. The mayor was interviewed and was relieved we could finally lay the matter to rest. He said now was a time to turn away from the negative and look forward. What couldn't survive would have to disappear. That's the way things had always been. Odda now faced the great challenge of getting the seeds of industry to sprout. In an attempt to reverse the trend of negativity they'd announced a competition to design a new logo for Odda.

Up by the Låtefoss waterfalls Samson Nilsen indicated and pulled over. I did the same and came to a halt behind a tourist coach. In the rear-view mirror I saw Nilsen get out and go over to what looked like a Nissan Sunny. I adjusted the mirror, but sunlight made it impossible to see through the windscreen. I started the engine and parked a little further down. With a hand raised against the sun I saw two heads inside the car. I still couldn't make out who the other person was. I got out and leaned against the Volvo. Eager tourists were taking pictures of the twin waterfalls. Some of the Japanese seemed ecstatic, putting their lives at risk by photographing in the middle of the road.

I remembered the accident that had happened years ago. One winter Sunday with the sun low we were on our way to the mountains and driving past Låtefoss. The drift from the falls had laid a sheet of ice across the road. My father lost control of the PV, the car spun and we ended up in the ditch. Frank was sitting in the front seat and got his face cut. Apart from that we were lucky. But I could still recall the fear as I got out to look at the damage. I sobbed and sobbed as my mother comforted me. It wasn't out of fear for either my brother or myself. I was afraid the accident would make us poor. The Volvo was proof that we had become affluent. Now we had lost everything.

I felt the movement from the passing cars and thought that statistically the same thing was bound to happen to some of the holidaymakers whizzing by. No matter what they did or where they drove, some of them would end up on their roofs or in the ditch.

After about fifteen minutes Samson Nilsen got out of the Sunny. He leaned down towards the side window and said something I couldn't hear. The words floated up into the air and dissolved. He got into the Audi and disappeared back in the direction of Odda. I waited until the Sunny started a couple of minutes later. We pulled out on to the road and drove at a reasonable speed down the valley. The traffic was thick and there was no chance of overtaking.

When we reached the centre of town, the Sunny stopped by the square. From a distance I saw a thin man get out and lock the car door. He was wearing a blue tracksuit. He had his back to me but I still recognised him immediately. Something inside my head clicked into place. Something moved into the groove. Without turning round Arthur Larsen crossed the square and went into Hamburger Heaven.

I waited a while before I followed.

Hamburger Heaven was Odda's gambling den. The windows were greasy, the smell of frying hung over the tables; you could have ordered a heart attack at the counter. On TV they'd turned gambling into family entertainment. The announcers were like smiling members of some cabin crew, and the lottery numbers were drawn at peak viewing time. In here everything had been stripped down to one basic aim: to prise as much money as possible from people who didn't have much. Except for a couple of places in Finnmark, Odda had the highest rate in the country of money per capita chucked away on gambling. Odda was the Atlantic City of Hardanger.

It was hot and stuffy inside the place that day. I sat down at the table next to Arthur Larsen. He filled out his coupons without looking up. I lit a cigarette and waited. Larsen wore a toupee, and it was the kind of toupee you noticed the moment you looked at him. The artificial hair was so unsuited to the man that it was difficult to think about anything else when you were near him. I'd interviewed the guy many times, most recently in connection with the foundry going bankrupt. He was one of the local union big shots who'd moved up through the system and ended up as foreman. Now he was in charge of administering the bankrupt estate, the only employee left at the place.

Larsen started when he saw me. I said nothing. He looked down again and carried on filling out his coupon, as though he hadn't seen me.

I went over to his table and sat down opposite him.

What did you want? I asked.

He stared at me and asked what I meant.

You rang me, I said.

I haven't rung you.

Maybe I'm wrong, but I think you rang me the other day.

No, I didn't ring.

Maybe you've forgotten. It wasn't much of a conversation. In fact, it was so short I couldn't place the voice until I saw you just now.

A guy wearing Roy Orbison glasses came over to the table. He was dressed in black and his hair was shaped with gel. He asked, wasn't there any horse racing today. Arthur Larsen answered that he didn't know about horses. Roy Orbison said there was nothing to know; the horse first past the post was the winner. Simple as that. You had to back the horse that was first past the post. Roy Orbison asked for a pen. No one had a pen. He went off to get one.

Why did you send me that video? I asked.

Arthur Larsen stopped writing.

You shouldn't get involved in all this stuff.

Get involved? You're the one who got me involved in it.

Can we meet somewhere?

Isn't this an okay place — apart from the smell of frying?

I can meet you in fifteen minutes.

Why did you send me the video?

Larsen didn't reply. He'd opened his tracksuit top almost down to his navel. I saw a few grey hairs on his birdlike chest.

You watched the video, right?

Yeah, but I've seen better films, I answered.

Larsen shook his head as if I was the biggest idiot in the world. He was probably right.

A young lad was killed, said Larsen. I wanted someone to find out what really happened.

And what did happen, really?

Larsen was silent. Roy Orbison had got hold of a pen and was on his way back. Larsen asked if I knew Elvebakken Café. He could be there in fifteen minutes. I said okay. Roy Orbison sat down at the table and filled out coupons. He explained that he always got Dally Arse wrong. He had the other horses all figured out, but in the last race here comes Dally Arse finishing like a storm and loses him thousands. He was certain they were doping Dally Arse. She wasn't that fucking good. They must have their own vet whose job it was to dope Dally Arse.

I went out into the light and headed over to the river.

The area next to the Shell station was called Elvebakken Café because drunks could drink in peace there. On rainy days they could shelter inside the cars that people had abandoned along the river bank. A gust of cold wind swirled up from the Opo. Melting snow over the last few days had caused the water to rise to a dangerous level.

I sat on the bonnet of an old Vauxhall and lit a cigarette. Across the river I saw the new cy50 factory that had begun production just a few months before the works went bankrupt. In front of that was the dicydianamide factory where my father got me a summer job when I was eighteen. I remembered summer nights out on the little balcony on the fifth floor where I used to watch the souped-up cars racing through the streets. I stood there in my dirty overalls and knew that I would not be a foundry worker like my father.

I waited a half-hour before ringing directory enquiries and getting Arthur Larsen's number. I had to sit inside the wrecked

Vauxhall because the roaring of the river made it impossible to hear. Larsen didn't answer. The bastard had tricked me. I rang Irene, but got no answer there either. I didn't know what to do next. I closed my eyes and listened to the roaring of the river.

I sat there in a Vauxhall which would never be going anywhere ever again.

35

Over in the car park Erik Bodd was sitting in my Volvo. He was eating a kebab and waved to me through the side window. I could see that in a few years' time he would be seriously overweight. He had a leaning towards it, just the way he had a leaning at the moment towards annoying people.

I bent down towards the passenger side window.

Excuse me, but what are you doing in my car? I asked.

I was thinking you might drive me out to the golf course, Bodd answered.

So that's what you were thinking. What else were you thinking?

Do you play golf?

I shook my head.

Pity, said Bodd. I thought we might play a round.

You think too much, I said.

You're right. I practise not thinking, and I practise not being at work. That's where golf comes into it. I put my golf bag on the back seat, by the way. Hope that's okay.

I didn't answer.

You should give it a try, said Bodd. You get hooked. Sometimes when I'm sitting at work, all I can think about is getting out for a game.

You shouldn't think so much.

I know, I can't seem to stop myself.

Now you can think about getting out of my car.

I opened the door and held it for him. Erik Bodd carried on sitting there. I carried on standing there. Bodd took hold of the door and closed it.

I've got a suggestion, he said. We drive out to the golf course. I play a round. You come with me.

I've got a better one, I said. You get out of my car.

Bodd turned and took his bag from the back seat. He pulled out an envelope, poked a photograph through the side window. It took a moment for me to identify the subject. The picture must have been taken with the lens poking between tree trunks. Two people sitting in a Volkswagen Beetle. Irene and me sitting in her car the night she broke it off. I stared at the picture. All I could think was how long ago it all seemed.

Small town, said Bodd.

I walked round the car and got in. I leaned my head against the headrest and put my hands on the wheel, as though I was about to take a driving lesson. Then I wiped the palms of my hands on my knees, started the engine, indicated and pulled into the road.

The first commandment for a journalist is to do your homework, Bodd said as we drove. People think they'll just stumble over stuff, but you have to do your homework. Take this golf course here. Who would have thought there was a golf course in Odda?

I didn't answer. All I could think was what an annoying voice the guy had.

I've only ever passed through Odda before, Bodd went on. It's nicer than I remember, but I could never live here. I don't know, I guess you get used to it. You can get used to the weirdest things.

He laughed.

Have you heard this one? They say Oddudlians have got so much heavy metal in them they have to be treated as dangerous waste.

I said nothing. I should have said they're called Oddites. I should have said he should have done his homework. I should have pulled over to the side, got the rifle from the boot and despatched the guy with a single shot.

We passed Tokheim and were out in Askane. I parked by the golf course. We sat in silence for a moment as the engine cooled.

Your story didn't quite add up, said Bodd.

What story? I asked.

Where you were that night. Your ex-wife and the flood in the basement. Have you got a better one?

I wondered if I should try to bluff. I was so tired of bluffing, but the last thing I wanted to do was tell Erik Bodd anything at all.

We climbed out of the Volvo. Bodd took his bag from the back seat. The golf course lay around the bay by the zinc factory. There was a view of pipes, tanks, depots and chimneys. The course actually floated on a pool of poison. They'd buried the old sins under a pile of earth and cobbled together an eight-hole golf course. People joked that when you picked your ball up out of a hole you risked losing half your arm.

I've played a lot of courses, said Bodd. But I think this one takes the biscuit.

He played a practice shot.

Know what? he said. I've been wondering what it's like to have your job. You work in a local office that they're seriously considering closing down. In a town that they're seriously considering closing down.

I didn't know whether to thank him for his concern or flatten him.

You're stranded here, aren't you?

It was humid. New clouds had formed over

the mountains in the south. In a few hours the heat would be transformed into thunderclouds. I'd read somewhere or other that the people who most often got struck by lightning were golfers.

Bodd leaned on his club.

Maybe she will turn up, he said. But I've worked on a lot of cases like this and most often they don't come back.

He looked at me.

I don't know what's happened, he said. Maybe you were secret lovers, maybe not. Whatever, there's bound to be rumours, and there's no defence against a rumour. If you decide to be open you can tell your story. Telling your story is actually a form of legal protection.

I wondered if it was Martinsen who'd taken the picture. It had to be Martinsen. But had he just happened to come across us, or had he followed me that evening? Why hadn't he said anything? And was it Martinsen who told Frank?

Erik Bodd said all I had to do was talk. He was a good listener. That was what he was best at. Listening. Hearing what others had to say. I thought that now the tables were turned. I was on the other side. I had become the fox they were hunting.

You can't blackmail me, I said.

I'm not blackmailing you, said Bodd. All I'm saying is what's best for you.

You've no fucking idea what's best for me.

Bodd swung his club and followed the flight of the ball. He nodded as he saw it land. He said he loved that sound. A club hitting a golf ball. Nothing could beat it.

We strolled down the fairway.

I've been trying to see a connection between the two cases, said Bodd as we walked along. The murder of the boy and the missing woman. But I can't do it. Maybe you can help me?

I wouldn't dream of it, I said.

Yes, that's one thing about Odda, said Bodd. Everyone here is so polite.

He stopped and looked at me.

Now listen. I understand you. In one-horse towns like this girls are always a tragedy. You have to fight for the best ones. And that one there was definitely a bit of all right.

He set off again. We reached the ball. Bodd looked at me.

Did you do away with her? Or maybe your brother did? It seems to me you would both have a motive. I've also heard rumours that your brother's the jealous type.

Oh yeah?

A little bird told me that your brother took all of his wife's clothes one evening and slashed them with a razor blade.

You're even sicker than I thought, I said.

He shrugged.

It's up to you. You decide, said Bodd. We're going to print the picture as soon as it's confirmed that Irene Bell is missing.

My first caught the side of his face, around the jaw. I hit him as hard as I could. Bodd fell backwards. For a moment he seemed small and pathetic as he lay there. Then he got up and dusted off his golfing trousers. He smirked, as though he were the one on top.

I turned and headed towards the car. A pain seared through my hand, but it seemed to me that it was worth it. I'd only done what I had to do. He'd said her name. He should never have said her name.

The picture still lay on the passenger seat in the Volvo. I put it in the glove compartment and started the engine. I indicated and drove off, thinking that Bodd was right about one thing. He was right that you can get used to the weirdest things. You accept all sorts of stuff, and you get used to it. Sooner or later it becomes your life.

36

A fat couple lay sprawled out on the lawn of the house next door. Their bodies glistened with oil. Yellow parasols were fastened to the sun beds. A radio bleated from the house. The fat couple lay quite still. They looked as if they were waiting to be barbecued or autopsied.

I took off my sunglasses and let myself in. Ronaldo was sitting on the sofa eating chocolate and drinking Coke. I asked how he was. He stared at the TV screen and didn't answer. There was a World Cup game on. Spain were leading Ireland 1–0. The Spanish never did well in championships. They seemed content to look good in front of the cameras.

In the bathroom I ran cold water over my hand. I wrapped a wet towel around my fist.

You be all right on your own for a bit? I shouted in to Ronaldo.

He still didn't answer.

You hungry? I called.

I went in and said I had to check something, then I'd fix us something to eat. I took the video cassette out of the player. I stood and watched the game. Damien Duff made a solo run that almost ended in a goal. I liked the Irish. They always played as if the world was going to end as soon as the final whistle blew.

I asked again if Ronaldo was hungry. He watched the game without looking at me. I shook his shoulder. Finally Ronaldo looked up.

You said we were going for a swim, he said.

Yes, I know.

Ronaldo picked up the Coke bottle but didn't drink.

You said we were going for a swim, he repeated.

We'll go for a swim later, I said.

I sat down in a chair and buried my face in the towel. Already the heat had made the towel lukewarm. My head seemed heavy in the soft cloth. I got up and told Ronaldo that he could come with me. He didn't budge.

I stood right in front of the television. He moved to one side to see. I turned off the television. He stared at the blank screen. I went over to him and took his arm. He tried to shake me off. I pulled him up. He struggled as I led him out into the corridor. I found his shoes and pressed them into his stomach.

Ronaldo gave me a defiant look and then

went into the living room. I followed and stood in the doorway. He turned the TV on again and wolfed more chocolate. I went over and snatched the chocolate from his hands.

If you want people to feel sorry for you, you can't be fat, I said.

Ronaldo didn't respond.

No one likes fat boys, I said.

I shook him.

Don't you realise you're in danger? I asked.

Ronaldo waited.

There's no one else looking out for you here, I said. I'm the only one looking out for you here.

What do you want? asked Ronaldo.

I didn't know how to answer. I didn't know what I wanted with him. I didn't even know if it was true that I was looking out for him. Maybe he was just the trump card I was holding on to without knowing why.

You don't want to be nice, said Ronaldo. You only want to be nice to yourself.

I shook my head, took the video and left. I swayed as I put on my sunglasses. The light was bright and blinding. Summer made the landscape look massive and swollen. I thought that summer was a sponge that sucked up everything around it.

My neighbour was sitting behind the wheel of my Volvo. Ask grinned through the side window as he licked at a toffee ice. I thought how for the second time in an hour someone had let himself into my car. I wondered why. Did they think I'd started up a taxi service?

Give me the keys, said Ask. We'll go for a little drive.

What's this about? I asked.

Nothing in particular, he said. I just feel like a little drive.

Ask was a couple of sizes too big for me to say no. I gave him the keys and jumped in. Ask started the engine and drove down towards the main road. He was sweating, as though he had a fever. He wiped his forehead.

Fine day, he said. But it's going to rain later on.

I couldn't recall the last time anyone other than me had driven the Volvo. The sun slanted in through the windscreen so that I could see the shadow of my own head moving along the fronts of the buildings and along the side of the road. As we drove towards the centre of town it jerked and jumped uneasily alongside us. Your head is such a fine shape, Irene had said to me one night. She had put her arms round me and asked whether anyone else had ever told me that. Only my mother, I had answered.

You should get yourself a better car, said Ask. You earn a pretty good wage, don't you?

I said this wasn't the right day to be talking about cars.

Ask breathed in heavily and wrinkled his nostrils.

Have you got a body hidden in the back of the car? he asked.

I stared at him.

He grinned: You're a man with a lot going on, right?

On the stretch before Kalvanes a cabriolet overtook us. Two girls were sitting up on the backs of the seats the way they do in American teen films. Their blonde hair flowed out behind them. The girls turned and waved. The driver sounded the horn.

Ask did the same, and sang: *Summertime and the living is easy.*

He turned towards me: Don't you think?

I didn't answer. Ask said Odda was a good place, but it was also a shit place. He said he liked to travel, but that he didn't earn enough.

You travel a bit in your job? asked Ask.

Get to the point, I said.

That is the point, he said. You always want something else. You always want something bigger. You wait for your lucky number to come up, see?

We were in the centre of town. A funeral cortege was moving along Røldalsvegen. I heard church bells. Ask pulled over and turned off the engine. The black hearse drove past. Then came Pedersen in the ice-cream van with a slew of cars behind him. Through the window of the ice-cream van I caught a glimpse of Pedersen's wife and his surly daughter.

Fucking ice-cream van, said Ask. Isn't that a bit much?

He probably wants to rack up the reading on his mileometer.

Eh?

Never mind.

That's fucking terrible, said Ask. Can't we live in peace, even here in Odda?

He drummed his fingers on the steering wheel. His keeper's hands were big and rough. He nodded at the video I still held in my hands. He said we could do a swap. On his video he had the most fantastic girls you could imagine. Last night he'd had twenty-four girls in less than an hour. Nurses, engineers, teachers, secretaries. Women who had every-thing. Women who just need a man, who are desperately searching for a man.

You're free as a bird, aren't you? said Ask. Or maybe not?

I stared at the cortege disappearing up the valley in the direction of the chapel.

It's all out there, said Ask. Why not help yourself?

234

What about Mumuki? I asked.

What about her? Do you fancy her?

I didn't answer.

That time I picked you up in Skjeggedal, it got me thinking how you and I could help each other. We're the perfect fucking pair. Know what I mean?

No.

I mean it in a good way. You drink-drive. Who doesn't? You mess around with women. Who doesn't? But you've got another life that not many people know about.

I said I still didn't understand.

I'm sure you do, said Ask. Think about it. Sleep on it.

Are you blackmailing me?

No. Wake up!

He whistled.

There's just so much I want to do, and I'm just a bit short of cash at the moment.

Forget it, I said.

I don't forget that easy, said Ask. I checked on the net to see how much you earn. And, put it this way, I got a pleasant surprise.

Forget it, I said again.

Hey. You seem a little cold for such a warm day, said Ask.

I didn't know if he was just trying it on, or whether he actually knew that Irene had disappeared. I wondered if the rumour had started to spread through Odda. It was the ideal place for gossip: big enough for things to happen, small enough for everyone to know about them. I wondered what kind of sum he had in mind. How much was love worth in Norwegian crowns?

Shouldn't we take a little drive up to Skjeggedal? Ask said and started the engine. Just to jog our memories?

Before he could pull out into the road I had opened the glove compartment and fished out the photograph. I showed it to Ask. He studied the picture of Irene and me sitting in the Volkswagen. It took a while for him to work out what it was.

Nice picture, he said as he handed it back.

It'll be in the papers soon, I said.

Ask sat back. Slowly it dawned on him what I was saying. He stared out of the side window. He chewed on his toffee ice. Then he ran a hand across his chin and his cheek. I was just waiting for him to hit out, just as I had hit out at Erik Bodd. He did nothing. Without another word he turned off the engine and climbed out. I watched him cross in front of the car and disappear down the street next to the hotel. A strange feeling of betrayal rose up in me. I was Ask's lottery ticket.

I hadn't come up.

37

Everything sticks to you when it's hot. There's no escape. You feel dirty. A film lies across your town, a layer of something clear and slippery that makes you feel uneasy. The town slips and slides while things attach themselves to you, make you heavy, so heavy that they drag you down.

I waited for the thunderstorm. The clouds in the south had fused into one enormous cloud. I thought maybe the rain would make things lighter. The mobile rang. It was Erik Bodd. He said he was writing up the story.

What story? I asked.

Your memory isn't up to much, said Bodd.

What story? I asked again.

He said he could read the story out to me. There were a few holes in it here and there, since I hadn't given him much to work on.

I want you to listen closely and correct any faults there might be, said Bodd.

I heard him talking about Irene. Something about me wanting her to be found alive. Something about how I would have to live with the suspicion, but that I was not guilty. It was a trick to get me to talk. The first draft of the story was so full of mistakes that any fool would try to correct the worst of them. If you did so, you'd be in shit up to your neck the day they were ready to publish the story.

I noticed a guy in a Saab on the other side of the street. He was staring at me as he ate an ice cream. I stared back. At that distance it was hard to see the expression on his face. I thought it must be that guy from *VG*.

Are you there? Bodd asked into my ear.

Yes, yes, I'm here, I said. I'm a good listener. That's what I'm best at.

Anything you want to change? asked Bodd.

Yes, there is one thing.

What's that?

Write that England have a goalkeeper problem. David Seaman is too old. Sooner or later Seaman's going to make a bad mistake.

I ended the conversation and crossed the street. I said hello to the guy in the Saab. He was wearing old-fashioned sunglasses and had nicotine-yellow teeth. He ate his ice cream slowly and methodically.

Do we have a problem? I asked.

Eh? he answered.

Do we have a problem? I asked again.

What do you mean?

Listen, I ask you a question, and you answer with another question. We're not getting anywhere. Do we have a problem?

Not that I know of.

Fine. For a moment there I thought we had a problem.

No problem.

Good.

The guy had finished his ice cream. The last drops trickled down his chin. His face was bright pink, as though he'd found himself on a Mediterranean holiday without suntan lotion.

You should put cream on, I said. Otherwise you'll get burnt.

What do you want? he asked.

A much better question is what do *you* want?

I think you're talking to the wrong man here, said the guy.

Maybe, but right now I'm going over to the Hardanger diner. After that I might go up to Hjøllo. Is that okay?

I don't think you're all fucking there, pal.

Oh no? Well at least now you know the details. Hardanger diner first, then Hjøllo. Not quite sure where after that. Have you got all that down? Maybe you'd like to come along with me?

The guy didn't say anything else. He seemed scared. He started his engine and roared away down the road. I went over to the Hardanger. They weren't open yet and I knocked on the window. Tor came over. He was bare-chested. I asked if he had five minutes. He let me in and he pulled me a beer. I took a first mouthful and thought how I shouldn't be drinking on an empty stomach.

Did you see the funeral procession? Tor asked. Who is it they've actually arrested?

Three Serbs, I answered.

But I saw one of them earlier today. The one called Dragan. He was definitely the one who was giving the Pedersen kid the most bother. So they haven't arrested him?

What do you mean? That they've arrested the wrong people?

I don't know. Maybe they just felt they had to arrest someone. So they picked up the first gang they came across.

That isn't quite the way it works, I said.

Then ring your brother and find out how it does work. Then you can also ask him why they haven't arrested the Reservist guys.

What for?

For setting fire to the hostel.

You think they set fire to the hostel?

Sure, what do you think?

I shrugged and asked him what he knew about Arthur Larsen.

Judas? said Tor.

Judas?

Yes. He's a floater. The type that always

rises to the surface.

He told me that everyone at the foundry had reckoned on Arthur Larsen's going full-time into politics. Then they would have been shot of him. Larsen had been offered the job of private secretary to the Employment Minister. People thought he would make an ideal guitar tuner for the minister who would be singing workers' songs from dawn till dusk. But Larsen had a sick wife at home, and the Labour Party lost the election.

Of course I'd been aware of Arthur Larsen's progress. The man had been made foreman at the works at the same time as a socialist took over as managing director. For the last few years Larsen had consistently argued the management's point of view and backed every new round of redundancies. He said the union should accept the sackings because it meant the rest of the workforce keeping their jobs. Naturally, in the end everyone got fired, and Larsen said that was acceptable because it meant he kept his job. Now he wandered around in there all by himself.

Can you understand that kind of person? Tor asked. One day they're sitting on our side of the table, the next they're smiling at us from the other side.

Is he a villain?

No, I don't think so. Maybe he's just the type of guy that sits on both sides of the table, someone you never know quite where to place.

I felt dizzy and raised my beer glass slowly. Smoke rose from the ashtray on the café table.

That's the way it fucking is now, said Tor. You've got fluctuating prices and wireless internet and global economy. You don't know your left from your right any more, can't tell good from bad, north from south.

Tor stubbed out his cigarette. He stood up and put on his cook's apron.

When you've got a managing director who's a socialist and a union representative who's his right hand it's a sure sign the owners intend to close the place down, he said.

I asked him if he thought the bankruptcy was planned.

Don't you think so? What do they want with a holding company and lawyers and Mister Fixits unless they're looking for a bankruptcy? asked Tor.

Before Christmas the American owners had given the managing director a golden handshake and sent Bobby Scott over from New Jersey. The Cohen Brothers company man lived in the suite at the Hardanger

Hotel; he looked like a grey office mouse but he ran up bar bills of around three hundred thousand crowns. Scott treated everybody and had a fling with several local girls. Every Monday morning he turned up clean-shaven at the office. At a meeting with the workers he'd told them they would be producing carbide in Odda for another hundred years. Four months later the bankruptcy was a fact.

Tor smirked: I never thought I'd hear myself say this, but it's a fucking shame they closed that factory. It was a shit place, the whole fucking thing, but it was our shit, know what I mean?

That's exactly what it was *not*, I said.

What do you mean?

It was the owner's shit. In the end not even your shit's your own.

True enough, said Tor and smiled.

He glanced at the clock up on the wall. He had to open the place up.

There are a lot of good people here, said Tor, but now everything's in the politicians' hands. And you know what that's like. It can work out well, or it can all go to hell.

Where does Arthur Larsen live? I asked.

In the apartment blocks at Nyland. What do you want with him?

We'll see.

Rumour says he's up to his neck in debt.

What kind of debt?

Pyramid.

Debt to who?

They say Samson Nilsen. But then they say so many things.

I thanked him for the beer and went back to my car. The afternoon sun seared down on my eyelids. I saw the mayor walking along the pedestrian precinct with a Somali. A camera team followed them as the pair walked in a stiff and unnatural way. At Glade Hjørna they were instructed to turn back and do it again. Over in the Lepers Park the TV2 guy sat there with the same fixed smile. He was talking into his mobile as he signed autographs for two little girls. At the parish church the priest was being interviewed by NRK. He stood behind the outside broadcast car with headphones on and a microphone stuck in his face. *Tell us!* it said along the side of the NRK car.

I drove up to Hjøllo while the priest preached about mercy on the car radio. A helicopter swung down the valley and drowned out the voice. In the rear-view mirror I saw a dark green Audi on my tail. I tried to see if it was Samson Nilsen driving. That would have made the perfect irony. First I tail him. Then he tails me. Up by Bøgarden I indicated left, while the Audi disappeared on up the valley in the afternoon light. My Volvo seemed more sluggish than usual. I liked the steering being a little heavy, that I had to wrestle with the wheel to make a turn. A car should give you a bit of a fight.

38

My father swore. At every missed chance another round of abuse. Normally he didn't swear. The bad language bubbled up out of him whenever he was watching football. When we were boys, the swearing created a bond between us. Our dad became another person. He was no longer just our father. He was someone we watched football with.

I asked if I could play a video for him. My father answered that he wanted to see the end of the match. Ireland had scored in injury time against Spain and they were playing extra time. They could cause a sensation even though they'd sent Roy Keane home. I glanced at the match, but everything was out of focus. My mother came down the stairs. She hugged me and asked if there was any news of Irene. She took me to one side and said she was afraid.

What d'you think has happened? asked my mother.

She's bound to turn up, I said.

I don't understand it. D'you think she's gone away somewhere?

I don't know, Mother. But I'm quite

certain she'll turn up again.

She stroked my arm and asked if I wanted something to eat.

You're getting so thin, she said.

I said no thanks and went back into the TV room. Ireland should have had the match sewn up in extra time but wasted all their chances. Half of them missed their penalties. My father swore again. We watched the summing-up from the studio before I fed the video into the player.

My father stared impassively at the amateurish recording. During a football match I could follow the play simply by observing him. The way he watched. The expression on his face. The curses that poured out. Now he was absolutely silent.

Do you want to see it again? I asked when it was over.

He shook his head.

I waited. I didn't want to say anything before I'd heard his response to the recording. He walked over to the cupboard and poured two whiskies. He handed one to me and sat down again. He didn't say a word. I thought he was trying to find some logic or system in what he'd seen, to work out the meaning of something that didn't quite hang together.

They're closing down the whole of Odda,

he said. They're closing down the whole of Odda and nobody cares.

He said you could go through an old telephone directory and cross out all the firms that didn't exist any more. All the offices that had closed down. All the government departments that had moved out. The hospital was all they'd managed to hang on to, but it could only be a matter of time before that was closed down too. That was the way to do it. Close it down one bit at a time. Dismantle it gradually. Wind the place up so slowly that no one even notices until it's all over.

My father drained his glass. He wiped his mouth before pinching the root of his nose between thumb and forefinger.

Where did you get this video? he asked.

From Arthur Larsen, I said.

He nodded, as though this fitted in with what he'd worked out.

They're dismantling the whole damn thing.

He said he'd heard of something similar happening in other places. The owner carries out a controlled winding down prior to gutting the factory. Before the terms of the bankruptcy were settled they'd dismantled and sold off most of the machinery.

But they can't steal a whole factory, I said.

Oh, can't they?

They're bound to be found out.

Maybe, maybe not. The trick is to steal what's valuable. You don't steal everything, only the stuff that's worth anything.

What about the creditors?

Who's interested in a bankrupt property with no assets? All that's left on the site now is scrap metal, poison and rubbish.

My father said he'd heard rumours of secret dealings involving the owners, Cohen Brothers, and their main competitor, the German firm Gedussa. The new managing director and a couple of Americans had apparently taken the trip to Frankfurt. Perhaps the American owners had found a buyer on the Continent.

Are you sure those are pictures of the foundry? I asked.

He nodded.

Well, then, this is proof, I said.

I don't know, said my father.

But someone knows what was in there.

So?

You're one of those who knows.

And who's going to ask me?

But somebody must speak out.

Not if they don't *want* to speak out. Or if they've been paid not to speak out.

What about Arthur Larsen?

What about him? Have you spoken to him?

I tried. He won't talk.

There was silence for a moment.

The truth is we're dying out, said my father. A whole town is dying out. You can understand a person dying, right? A guy drowns, a mother dies of cancer. But you can't understand a whole town dying.

I stood up and asked where the holes in the fence were. My father stared at me and asked why I wanted to know. I shrugged. He described where the holes were. I headed for the door. He followed.

You know what happened on the last day at work? he asked.

I nodded. I'd written a short piece about it. The workers had been laid off with immediate effect. No one was allowed to take work clothes, helmet or other gear with them. On the way out of the gates for the last time everybody had been searched by security guards.

My father pressed his index finger against my chest.

If the crime is big enough, you get away with it, he said.

I went out on to the grass. That dense thundercloud had almost reached the sun and darkened the afternoon. Soon it would rain. I drove into the centre and parked by the Co-op Megastore. I got out and crossed the road by the kebab place. From the

250

pedestrian precinct I went down an alleyway. I found the hole in the barbed wire and waited a while until I was sure no one was following me. Then I slipped through.

The whole foundry site was covered in a fine film of chalk dust. It made the buildings and warehouses look deep-frozen. I walked slowly past the gatehouse, the baths and the carpentry shop. I didn't know where to start looking. Every time I went into the place it struck me how big the site was. As children we were never allowed inside the gates, even though our father worked there. It was a world to which we had no access.

Each morning I'd woken to the sparking and grinding of the factory. Now the place was so quiet I could hear my own breathing. An almost translucent curtain of rain was working its way down the valley. Beyond the factory site the town was busy. I heard traffic, hammering, children shouting, an electric lawnmower. I thought how the foundry was a town within a town. There were buildings, gates, railway lines. Everything was abandoned, as though after a war or a natural disaster. The factory was a dead town inside a dying town.

I walked past the cyanamide factory towards the foundry itself, where my father used to work. The enormous building was scorched and blackened. I remembered something my father said once about the size of the foundry. How small it made you feel. You were nothing. You couldn't control those powers. The energy, the heat, the mass. He'd said there was something good about it, too. In order to succeed, and to take control, you had to find your place. And if you found your place, suddenly you were everything.

I walked around the enormous furnace that was ringed by small rail tracks carrying crucibles. Sunlight shafted in here and there. Then suddenly it grew much darker. I guessed it had clouded over completely. I thought how my father's town was not the same as mine. This was his, this town that lay within the town. Now it was as though all the power had drained out of the buildings. The rooms had lost control. An Odda calendar hung crooked in the duty room. There were still coffee cups on the table. Two helmets on a shelf. A car magazine tossed down on the floor. A poster urging people to join the May Day parade.

The rain had started. The drops hit the roof and were visible between the pillars outside the foundry. There was a sudden flash of lightning, and then a rumble of thunder. I counted the seconds between the flash and the rumble. I wondered if it was true what they said, that in a small town villains look like heroes. You can't know in a small town. You think you know, but you can never know.

Maybe my father had been right, maybe not. It might be part of his grieving; that was probably what lay behind his conspiracy theories. But he seemed very certain. Maybe people still worked there at night, dismantling the factory, as though working some final, illegal night shift. Maybe it was such grand larceny that it was possible to get away with it. Maybe they'd be reported to the police, or to the Monopolies Commission, but it seemed impossible to find any traces of theft here. The case would probably be dropped after a few months.

Moreover, the guilty parties were over on the other side of the Atlantic. Cohen Brothers had sold off the contract. They'd laid off the workers. Finally, they had probably cleaned out the guts of the factory, taken the heart out of the heartland in more or less the same way as the rich steal body parts from the poor.

I stood quietly up on the scaffolding. Directly beneath me I could hear footsteps. Someone was inside the foundry. I was no longer alone. I was trying to work out what to say if a guard or someone found me there. I couldn't think of anything sensible. There was no good explanation for my being there.

Then a form detached itself from the shadows below me. A deer appeared just ten metres from me. He ambled over to the carbide oven. I'd heard that there were foxes running around inside the place, but I didn't know that deer were here too. I guessed this was a young buck sheltering from the thunder and lightning. I walked out further along the scaffolding. The deer turned towards me. He didn't look nervous or afraid. He just stared at me, breathing quickly and rhythmically.

39

The apartment blocks up in Nyland looked deserted, but curtains twitched as I headed for the external staircase. I caught a glimpse through a window of grey hair and a nose pressed against the glass. *Vibeke and Arthur* it read on the neighbouring door. I rang the bell. No one opened up. Somewhere a radio was playing, but I couldn't work out whether it was from Arthur Larsen's or one of the neighbours'.

I was surprised to find he lived here. The company had built these four blocks in the fifties for the workers. People immediately christened the area 'Chicago'. Now the council owned most of the flats and had filled them with pensioners, immigrants and the unemployed. The rubbish bins overflowed and the stairwell stank of shit.

The rain had eased off a bit. Soon it would clear up again. A soaking wet dog came padding down the corridor. It shook itself and stared at me, as though it thought we could be friends. I tried the door. The handle was warm. I entered the hallway and waited. Nothing happened.

I carried on into the living room. Sweat sprung up on my neck. A drop ran down my spine. The room had the sickly smell of sleep, dust and medication. A clock on the wall was ticking. I looked at the pictures, the books, the ringbinders.

From a room further down the corridor I heard muted sounds. I approached a bedroom door that was ajar. Sitting on the bed with her back to me was an amazingly fat woman. She was wearing a nightgown, and her body looked overproportioned, as if she had been assembled from numerous heavy layers. Strewn around her on the bed were stuffed toys. I saw a bear, a dog, a lion, a giraffe. The woman turned slowly towards me, but her eyes were covered by one of those sleeping masks they give you on long-distance flights.

Arthur? said the woman.

I couldn't take my eyes off all those layers of fat. I stood there thinking her whole body had to be full of fat. Underneath was nothing but layer after layer of fat all the way into the skeleton.

Arthur? she said again.

She moved her hands in the direction of the sleeping mask and I backed away with the feeling that I had seen something I wasn't meant to see.

I was back in the living room when Arthur Larsen came down the stairs from the floor above. He was wearing shorts and a T-shirt. There was something wrong, something that didn't quite add up. Then it dawned on me that he wasn't wearing his toupee.

The fat woman in the bedroom let out a howl. Larsen just stared at me before hurrying past. I didn't know what to do, so I sat down at the kitchen table and lit a cigarette. I stared out through the dirty windows. The view was of the public baths and the foundry.

A few minutes later Larsen came back. He went over to the sink and filled a tumbler of water. He put some ice in the glass, then disappeared again. Shortly afterwards he returned and got himself a glass of water. He sat at the table without looking at me.

Larsen moistened his lips with his tongue and spoke in a low voice.

You're the first person to have seen her in ten years, he said. She's so big she can't get out of the room.

It was strange seeing him without his toupee. It was as if he'd been another person and was now himself again.

I love her, he said. Can you understand?

I nodded. The nod was a lie, but it was the simplest lie in the world.

Do you understand? Larsen asked again, as though he had caught me out in the lie.

Yes, I said.

No, you don't. You find it unbelievable, don't you?

I waited.

You think she's the fattest woman you've ever seen. You think, how could anyone love a woman as fat as that?

He was right. I didn't understand it. I'd seen his wife, and all I'd seen was the fattest woman in the world.

I put my cigarette out and said: I waited half an hour for you over by the river. Don't you think you owe me an explanation?

Larsen said nothing. I asked if he could give me some kind of explanation. He raised the glass to his lips, but it was empty and the ice cubes clinked against the rim.

Maybe I can help you get started? I said.

Larsen was staring at a point far away. He sat with his arms dangling and his face empty.

Here's what I know, I said. Correct me if I'm wrong.

I got no response.

Let's say someone's been stealing parts of the foundry, I said. And let's say someone has dismantled the most valuable bits before the assessors have been in to value the assets. They've dismantled machinery, engines and equipment and loaded up several wagons with it or else moved it down the fjord.

Still Larsen said nothing. I couldn't figure him out. He'd sent me the video. He wanted me to know. But he didn't say a word.

Maybe the whole lot's been shipped to Germany, I said. Maybe some other country. But let's stick with Germany. Or should we try somewhere else? How about Poland, for example?

Larsen picked up one of the ice cubes and slipped it into his mouth.

Let's suppose everything goes according to plan, I went on. The factory is stripped of its valuables. All that's left is rubbish. Everything's going fine, the thieves can work away well hidden. It's all swimming along, until suddenly something happens. I don't know what. The end result, anyway, is that a young lad is forced off the road.

I waited.

Does any of this seem familiar? I asked. Is that the way it happened? The boy posed a threat to someone and was forced off the road. Maybe it wasn't intentional. Maybe the idea was just to scare him. But suddenly it wasn't just robbery any more, now it was murder.

Larsen asked if I had a cigarette. I gave him one and lit one myself. My forehead was sweating, my throat and my palms. I longed for a shower.

Did you lose your nerve? I asked. Maybe you're a thief, but you're no murderer. You sent me that video so that I would stir things up a bit. Did you make it to cover yourself?

I waited.

Larsen was about to say something when the fat woman shouted from the bedroom. It was as though her voice came from a radio, or from some place far away. Larsen got up and disappeared. I stayed where I was and smoked. I opened the kitchen window to let in a little fresh air. My shirt was still damp with sweat and rain. I heard the sounds of Chicago. Coughing. Whistling. Banging. A dog. Heavy footsteps out in the corridor. A car starting outside the block.

I took out my mobile and listened to my messages. Most were from journalists who wanted me to get in touch or else suggested different ways I could spin my story. *Aftenposten* wanted to do a profile of me. A TV crew were making a documentary about Special Branch and wanted to talk to me.

None of the messages were from Irene.

I thought of that night when I had asked her what was the best experience we had shared. She had laughed and refused to answer. I'd asked her why. Then you'd know

260

how I think, she'd said, I'd make it too easy for you. And she'd turned the question around and played it back to me. My answer was that I had nothing to lose, she already had a hold on me. I could tell the plain truth.

I'd told her that the best of all was that morning we had stood outside the swimming pool in Trieste. The smell of chlorine was so strong. A morning mist hung over the quays and boats glided by in the drizzle. We'd looked in through the window and seen a group of pensioners exercising in the pool. Laughing, we'd gone through the same motions in the rain outside. Irene had leaned against me and said she wanted to grow old with me.

40

By the time Larsen returned his cigarette had almost burnt to ash. He sat down and picked up the butt, inhaled and blew out a cloud of smoke. I offered him the pack but he declined. He looked at me.

China, he said.

China?

The gear's going to China.

Oh yeah?

Larsen began talking. He spoke slowly, as though each sentence had to be built from the ground upwards. He said some of the gear had been moved in trailers and some by boat. First to Germany, then on to China. There was an agreement between the American owners and their German competitor. The Germans operated a foundry in China that was almost identical to the one at Odda.

So Cohen Brothers deliberately ran the factory down? I asked.

That's what some people would say, said Larsen.

And what would you say?

Looking at it now it seems as though they'd

decided even before they took over.

And you were their sell-off boy?

Larsen waited a few moments.

You like to think you matter, see? he said. You think you've got the experience and the insight to steer things in a certain direction. I was convinced that a degree of rationalisation at the factory would mean more saved jobs.

No way it could, I said. So after that it was just a question of stripping the corpse?

It's easy to be wise after the event, said Larsen. But even that is a kind of wisdom, isn't it? I didn't see it then, but now I can see that it might easily look as though they used me. In the end I had no choice.

Oh no?

To cut a long story short: I don't know any more when it began or when it ended. Whatever, I got into a kind of panic when that lad was forced into the river. I suppose the most I can say is this: that I wanted someone to find out what really happened.

Larsen looked at me.

I wanted you to find out, he said.

Larsen said it slowly, as though it needed time to seep through to me.

It's the police's job to find out things like that, I said. Why didn't you go to the police?

Larsen didn't answer. He fetched himself another glass of water.

263

Were you scared of getting involved? I asked.

I had no way of knowing who was involved, he said.

How come?

Larsen said that a couple of months before the bankruptcy was filed the council had given the foundry a bridging loan of twelve million crowns. It was part of a rescue package, to keep the place going. The company deliberately misled the council.

I couldn't know who was involved to make it look like something other than a very high-risk loan, Larsen said. Or even who wound up with the money in the end.

Who do you think it was?

I don't know. And I'm not going to guess either. This is a small town, and I want to be able to go on living here.

He smiled.

I can't go, and I can't stay, he said.

And the money was used to buy people? I said.

Some went to organisation and transport, said Larsen. Some went to those who actually did the physical work.

And some to you?

You've seen her, said Larsen. She's ill. I needed the money.

Sick people get help in this country, I said.

Not her, said Larsen.

He drank. It made me thirsty to watch him drinking. I asked what he and Samson Nilsen had talked about up at the Låtefoss waterfalls. Larsen seemed surprised. He hadn't reckoned on my knowing about Samson Nilsen.

Nothing much, said Larsen.

I said it seemed a bit much to drive all the way up to Låtefoss just to exchange a few words about the nice summer weather. Larsen said nothing.

You owe him money, don't you? I asked.

What do you mean?

I mean that Samson Nilsen is a one-armed bandit. Of the type it's very easy to get addicted to. It's easy to kid yourself that a lot of money's going to come pouring out of a man like that.

I don't understand you.

This stuff about your wife not getting any help. Samson Nilsen's got you by the balls. You owe him for gambling debts, isn't that right?

Larsen paused. Then he said he'd invested some money in a company. He was aware of the risk, but believed in the company. It wasn't the usual pyramid operation.

No, of course not, I said. They never are.

I looked at Larsen and thought he must be the loneliest man in Odda. Closing down the factory might have saved him his job, but in the process he had lost all his friends. And now here he sat in this apartment block with a big fat debt and a big fat wife.

I know what you're thinking, said Larsen.

And what am I thinking?

That I'm not much of a man.

I'm thinking more about what happened to principles.

What do you mean?

What happened to social democracy, what happened to solidarity.

Sometimes you can't afford to have principles, said Larsen.

I shook my head.

What's Samson Nilsen's involvement in this? I asked.

He was the co-ordinator, Larsen replied. He had the local knowledge and the contacts.

You suggested him to the owners?

Larsen nodded.

And who did the actual physical work? I asked.

People from the hostel. Asylum seekers.

Nice bunch, I said.

It was Samson Nilsen's said Larsen.

He said they were good workers. They could work at night, and knew how to keep quiet about what they were up to. If they did start talking it would only work against them in the end.

Did they use the Serbs? I asked.

Them too, said Larsen.

Larsen's wife called out from the bedroom. She seemed uneasy. Larsen got up. He looked out of the window.

What are you going to do with this? he asked.

What would you do? I said, and thought how Larsen had backed the wrong horse. He had wanted me to stir things up a bit, but I was too deep in shit myself.

What actually happened about the Pedersen kid? I asked.

Samson Nilsen must have thought he was a threat, answered Larsen.

A threat to who?

Larsen's wife called again. She seemed almost despairing.

You better go now, said Larsen.

He looked at me before disappearing into the bedroom. I finished my cigarette. Then I got up and walked over to the sink. Greedily I swigged down four or five glasses of water. Outside it had stopped raining. The evening sun crawled slowly across the mountains. Looking down from the outside corridor I saw neither journalists nor anyone else who might be tailing me. The cars parked along outside the blocks looked perfectly normal, as though they belonged here. It was a quiet evening. The rain had sharpened the smells of summer.

I was walking along the corridor when I heard Larsen's voice. He came up to me. He was wearing his toupee now.

If you write about this, will you keep me out of it? he asked.

I didn't answer.

I can't get involved in it, he said.

So you think you're not involved already?

There was a silence between us.

Everything I did, I did it for her, said Larsen.

41

The anti-racism demonstration made its way down Røldalsvegen. It passed directly in front of me as I watched it through the windscreen. All the same it was as though I was watching it from a distance. Elvestad the mayor was in front, along with the priest and a black man I'd never seen before. There must have been at least three or four hundred people taking part. Some carried torches. All the time I sat in an uncomfortable position because I didn't want the back of my wet shirt to stick to my spine.

Once the demo had passed I drove on. Cars approached and blended together. Outside the street began to dissolve. My head felt as soft as the asphalt under the tyres. At the crossroads by the Smeltar I passed my brother. Frank was driving one of the new police cars and made a left turn without seeing me. I could have reached out and touched him.

At McDonald's I bought some hamburgers to take back for Ronaldo. When I came out again I saw Martinsen on the other side of the quay. He was watching me from a metallic Peugeot. I walked across to him.

Quiet day today? I asked.

What? replied Martinsen.

Not much to do? You need days like that now and then. Just take it real easy. Sit there and watch life flowing past. Take a picture now and then.

Martinsen said nothing.

I waited.

What do you want? asked Martinsen.

Nothing special. I just like to have a bit of a natter now and then. By the way, do you know if anybody else is tailing me?

Tailing you?

Yes, tailing.

No.

Maybe you don't take enough interest?

Well, it's a tough job, said Martinsen. I nod off now and then.

Not all the time, I said. Sometimes, you're very sharp indeed.

I got back in the car and drove out towards Tokheim. Martinsen followed me. Then *VG* in a grey Mercedes. Then someone else who was also tailing me. I couldn't quite see who it was. All I knew was that I was flavour of the month.

Ronaldo wasn't at home. The only trace of him was the Coke bottle on the table and the chocolate wrapper on the sofa. I ate one of the hamburgers as I stood by the window. I wondered where Ronaldo was. He couldn't be far away. I rang Irene and got no answer. I thought how everything was drifting away from me. Everything I loved disappeared and was gone.

I drove round looking for Ronaldo. At the floating jetty I found the mother duck with her single surviving duckling. She seemed agitated and was giving the duckling a scolding. A few gulls circled over the surface of the water. On the radio I'd heard the experts saying that gulls had become more aggressive in recent years. The experts couldn't explain it, but gulls were getting more and more aggressive.

At the Hjøllo bridge I parked and walked down to the river. Martinsen and the others were no longer on my tail. They'd probably given up. Maybe I wasn't such a big deal after all. The water level must have risen in the course of the day. Dean Martini sat in his armchair and drank from a bottle. If the river kept rising at the same rate he'd soon find himself homeless. I walked over to him, said hello, asked if he'd seen a boy in a football shirt.

Are you a priest? asked Dean Martini.

No, I'm not a priest.

You look like a priest. Are you married?

No.

Priests are allowed to get married. You know that?

I know that.

Just go ahead and get married, even if you are a priest. Get married and have dozens of kids. On you go.

Martini got up and walked over to me.

What's your name? he asked.

Robert, I answered.

Robert? said Martini.

He leaned in close to me and looked me straight in the eye. He reeked of alcohol.

I only know one Robert, Martini said in a low voice. The guy who ran off with my wife.

It wasn't me, I said.

Are you married, priest?

No, I said, and pulled away from him.

I walked further on down the river. Over on the far bank was where the factory used to dump its shit. In my childhood the lorries shuttled back and forth across the bridge to empty the waste along the river bank. The slag heaps had altered the landscape where I grew up. Thousands of lorryloads over the years had completely changed the topography. I thought that now my own personal topography was changed, and it had taken only a few days.

I recalled a film in which the leading

character was in love with a woman he never won. Years later he reflected on the fact that love is always about being in the right place at the right time. Many times I'd wondered what might have happened had I stood up just a few seconds earlier that New Year's Eve, and asked Irene to dance.

I carried on to the mouth of the river but saw no sign of Ronaldo. On the offloading quay I stood smoking in the evening heat. Everything was quiet. Odda seemed a million miles away. In the old days there was always some action at least three times a day: six in the morning, two in the afternoon, ten at night. That's when they changed shifts at the factory, and the streets would be filled with cars. Now the long day was over. The foundry was history. The only sounds came from the river as it pumped water out into the fjord, like blood from an open wound.

I had worked out that Guttorm Pedersen must have been forced into the river because he'd tried to blackmail Samson Nilsen. It was about money. It was always about money. Maybe Samson Nilsen had only meant to scare the boy. Maybe the lad had lost control of his car. He wasn't, after all, a speedway driver like Nilsen. I didn't know.

I flicked the butt into the river and went over to my office. I opened the window and

273

felt the mountain air flowing in over my face. I turned on the computer and waited. I began to write. I wrote quickly. I wrote down everything I knew. I wrote down everything I thought I knew. When I was through, I looked over what I had written. Here and there I'd had to guess, but the words did convey some kind of sense.

The owners, Cohen Brothers, must have planned a controlled running-down of production at the foundry. With bankruptcy approaching they'd put Samson Nilsen in charge of gutting the factory before the creditors moved in. Nilsen was the right man. He was a fixer and a trickster. Making money was what he did. Asylum seekers had done the physical work. A cheap workforce that could be relied on to keep quiet. They stripped the place of its assets, working by night. They dismantled motors, machines, cranes, computers. The stuff was taken away in lorries or else freighted down the fjord in cargo ships.

Everything was going all right until someone found out what was going on. It was all going along nicely until Guttorm Pedersen stumbled across the theft. Maybe Samson Nilsen was using him as labour too. Maybe he'd followed the Serbs one night and discovered the truth that way. The lad was a racist and suddenly he was in possession of information that he wanted to exchange for money. The asylum seekers were worried because they risked being thrown out of the country. Samson Nilsen was worried because the Pedersen kid couldn't be trusted. He went to see the lad, had a word with him, tailgated him to frighten him a bit. It went wrong. Guttorm Pedersen was forced off the bridge and into the river.

I stood up and closed the window. I thought how I could send the story in now, but I knew no one would believe me. I was certain that this was pretty well what had happened. All the same, they would never print the story. I'd found out what had happened, I'd arrived at a kind of truth, but Bergen would call and ask me for my sources; they would want to know if I could prove what I had written.

And I couldn't. I couldn't, for example, prove that Samson Nilsen had dumped his own Subaru in the fjord. I was certain he'd done it to hide his tracks after the incident involving the two cars. All things considered, Samson Nilsen was a tight-fisted bastard — he'd even reported the car stolen to get the insurance money. The same day he, or someone, had stolen the Serbs' BMW, driven it up to Eitrheim and torched it. Nilsen knew the wreck would be found; he knew that everyone would assume the Serbs were behind it. They'd think the Serbs had forced their tormentor into the river. They'd had enough of the Pedersen kid and made an end of it. Three asylum seekers would end up inside on suspicion of the murder of a Norwegian boy. People would relish it.

I rang the desk editor. She answered at the first ring. I said who it was. She was silent.

There's just one thing, I said.

And what's that? she asked.

We've got a loose cannon on board, I said.

What d'you mean?

We've got a loose cannon on board here.

Who is it?

You know that as well as I do. I should have mentioned it earlier.

The desk editor sighed.

I really think you should take a bit of sick leave, she said.

I just thought I'd tell you, I said.

Thanks, she said and hung up.

Once again I read over what I had written. Then I closed the document. The computer asked if I wanted to save it.

I clicked No.

42

I was gin without the tonic. I was a fish with no fjord. A suit without a man. The bartender shook me and said I couldn't sleep here. I explained that he was looking at the remains of a dissolute life.

The journalists were crowded together around a table by the window. I heard TV2 saying she'd been interviewed by Channel 24. NTB had done a profile of Old Beardy from *Folkebladet*. *Dagbladet* said that if you looked at it statistically more people were murdered in Odda than in Oslo. NTB said he was sick to death of Odda. He wanted to go home. *Aftenposten* glanced over at me. I raised my glass to him.

Erik Bodd came in and walked up to the bar. I was delighted to see he had a plaster on his nose.

Good evening, Chinatown! I said.

He smiled at me, as though I were the best company imaginable.

All right? asked Bodd.

I'm as lit up as a Christmas tree, I answered.

What're you doing here?

I like to watch people drinking.

Bodd laughed. Then he touched his nose.

Sorry about what happened earlier, he said. You know how it is. Is there anything I can do for you?

Such as what? You've already done so much for me.

The fact of the matter is that I do care, said Bodd. I'm good at that.

I didn't think they made them like you any more, I said.

If there's anything I can do just let me know.

You're so kind. Let me give you a kiss.

Bodd laughed as the barman handed him his beer. He said I should get in touch. I answered that I would give his offer careful consideration. I wondered if Bodd was the type who had to get knocked down before he respected someone. I considered knocking him down again, so that he would have even more respect for me.

Bodd went over to join the others. He said something that made them all laugh. It was so damn funny. The journalists sat over there and thought they knew everything. They knew nothing. People wanted the truth. People wanted to read things that were true. And what did they get? Sickness, death, accidents, divorces, gossip.

Soon the newspaper vans would be out on their rounds. The black smudge would be smeared open on tables everywhere and people would have something nice to go with their coffee. The Irene story. I stuck a cigarette in my mouth and thought of all those stories. The people who disappeared. For a few days the newspapers were full of stuff about a particular story. You got all the details. You found out all about the missing person and the last known movements of the missing person. For a while you remembered the name, the place, the suspects. Then some shit happened somewhere else in the country. The journalists all headed off there like some touring company and you never got to hear the end of the first story. I loved Irene. I really loved her. In print it would look like the simplest thing in the world.

I got up and made my way over to the journalists. I asked if they had enjoyed their stay. No one answered. I asked if there was anything else they'd been wondering about? Did they want me to round up some village idiots for them to interview? I knew this place like the back of my hand. Did they want to see the back of my hand? Maybe they wanted to photograph it?

Perhaps I could take them to the fields by the river? A white-throated nightingale had been seen there. A rare bird. Make a great subject. If they could get a picture of the white-throated nightingale they could win prizes and stuff. You only saw the white-throated nightingale about once every twenty or thirty years. I was staring at Martinsen as I said this. He looked away. I was making a fool of myself and he couldn't bear to watch.

There was silence round the table.

Yes, you know where to find me, I said, and went back to the bar.

I ordered another whisky. The bartender poured the drink reluctantly and put it on a mat in front of me. There was laughter from the journalists' table. Someone was being dangerously funny. I smelt my suit jacket. I smelt of sweat and crap, but at least it was my own crap. In the mirror between the glasses I saw my face. I looked pale and sensitive. A white-throated nightingale. A rare bird.

Blue light was tossed into the bar. I turned and saw an ambulance driving past. The journalists got out their mobile phones. I got up from the bar stool and went out into the street. The night sky arched above me. The heat still hung in the air. I felt the pavement under my feet. I walked along the harbour promenade. A police car drove past, and in a brief moment I saw myself sitting in the back seat. I walked faster. I began to run. People were crowding round the floating jetty. The ambulance with its blue light flashing was parked close by.

The yellow Brazil shirt was visible between the curious onlookers. A man was leaning over the small body. I shouted for them to let me through. Someone held me back. They put the boy on to a stretcher and carried him to the ambulance. As they ran with the stretcher I saw how the head lolled.

I went over to the ambulance and was stopped by a guy in a red jacket.

Who are you? he asked.

He couldn't swim, I answered.

The guy held me by the shoulder and looked into my eyes.

Have you been drinking? he asked.

I'm the father, I said.

Okay, you can come, he said.

The guy opened the rear doors of the ambulance and told me to hop in. Ronaldo lay lifeless on the stretcher. Water dripped from his hair and his shirt. Several tubes were connected to his body. There was a harsh smell in the ambulance and I thought that this was the smell of the fjord, this was the smell of bad things. We drove through Odda at high speed. Beyond the swaying windows I caught glimpses of a wash of light, as though I were sitting in a radio car at the funfair and the world was spinning round until everyone was dizzy and happy.

Up at the hospital they took Ronaldo out and wheeled him in through the automatic doors. I stood there a moment. Then I went in. The world closed behind me. A nurse took me by the arm. She spoke Swedish.

You can come along, she said.

I followed her down the corridor. She disappeared and came back with a mug of coffee. I took a swig.

I was going to teach him to swim, I said.

Oh yes?

Today. We were going to go to the baths. And I was going to teach him to swim.

She stared at me.

You're his father?

I nodded.

We'll need some information about your son, she said.

She fished out a notebook. I drank from the mug.

What is the boy's name?

I hesitated. She looked up.

What is the boy's name?

I don't know, I said.

You don't know?

No.

She took me by the arm and said it was best if I sat down. I did as I was told. Light flooded from the strip lighting on the ceiling, harsh and white.

Is he going to die? I asked.

You'll be able to talk to the doctor later, she said. But he's in a critical condition.

She said there was something she had to do. She would let me know as soon as there was any news. I sat down in a chair. It was a black chair. The lift was stationary. Then it went up three floors. And came down again. Then it stood still. I sat in the chair. The lift stood still. The chair was black. I sat in the black chair. I pressed my forehead against my hands as I slowly sobered up.

Finally I got up and walked over to the window. Down below the river was swollen. The river split and flowed past Øyna with a roar. Irene was waiting for me in the car. We had made love in that car. Now she opened herself to me again. She was smoking, and wearing her white summer frock. We kissed and floated up into the air as the landscape floated away from beneath us. We rose into the warm night, rose over the trees, over the river, over the islands, over the streets.

The nurse patted my back.

You can see him now, she said. The doctor will come and have a word with you afterwards.

Ronaldo was in Intensive Care. A breathing

machine had been connected up. Tubes going in and out of him. His pulse and blood pressure were shown on a screen. The nurse checked the cables, the piss bag, his heartbeat. Ronaldo's upper half was bare. His hands lay still on the duvet. His face looked illuminated in the faint light. His eyes were closed.

Shall we bring in another bed? asked the nurse.

His name is Ronaldo, I said.

I lay my hand on his forehead. I stroked his hair. He felt cool in the warm room.

It's me, I whispered. Dad's here now.

43

It was strange the way the houses disappeared. The streets beneath me pulled away. In the rear-view mirror I watched the lights of Odda getting smaller and smaller. The Volvo was standing quite still as the town moved. Odda was approaching at high speed and the engine wasn't even on. Not until up by Hovden did the town brake and come to a halt.

I heard laughter and music from the Bruce villa. Several cars were parked in the driveway. I took the rifle out of the boot and walked up the gravel path. I rang the bell. Nothing happened.

I knocked. A small man wearing horn-rimmed glasses and a dinner jacket opened the door. I didn't know him. The guy must have been well away because he didn't even notice I was holding a rifle in one hand. He said hello and smiled, as though I were the final guest they had been waiting for.

Inside there was a buzz of voices. My head was grating. A couple sat close together on the sofa. Through the French windows I saw people dancing. A group was playing by the swimming pool. I recognised them as the local blues band. They'd simply exchanged their denim jackets for dinner jackets.

Samson Nilsen stood at the top of the stairs with a drink in his hand. People around him were laughing. I crossed the floor and headed for the stairs. I must have been the invisible man, because no one made any attempt to stop me. Once I became visible again Samson Nilsen raised a hand.

Don't do anything silly, he said.

I said nothing. Samson Nilsen seemed calm. He thought he was in control of the situation. It irritated me.

He nodded towards a room along the corridor.

Perhaps we might go in there so we don't disturb the others?

I don't think they have any objection to being disturbed, I said.

Samson Nilsen handed his drink to a woman in a blue dress, as though he were preparing for something or other. His hair was combed back, and it occurred to me that he would be bald soon. He looked good now, but his widow's peak showed he was receding and in a few years' time he would be more or less bald.

What's this about? asked Nilsen.

You know perfectly well.

No, I must admit I haven't a clue.

I turned round for a moment. From the Bruce villa there was a perfect view of Odda. You could see the fjord and the lights from the town. The band was still playing out in the garden. I thought I saw the mayor dancing with a blonde girl. People were chatting and laughing in the rooms. It irritated me. It was as though I wasn't there. It was as though I wasn't holding a rifle in my hand.

I turned towards Samson Nilsen again.

I don't know what the fuck to do with you, I said.

Oh really, he said.

Got any suggestions?

What's on your mind, Bell?

How to punish you. How to hurt you.

I still don't know what all this is about.

He couldn't swim, I said. He couldn't fucking well swim.

Who are we talking about here?

Did you push him off the floating jetty?

I haven't pushed anyone.

Samson Nilsen shook his head.

I pressed the rifle hard into his stomach. A convulsion shook his body before he composed himself and looked at me with contempt. I took a step back. I thought how I wanted to shoot him, but my hatred was weak and useless.

I said: You think you can get away with this?

Suddenly I was unsure myself. Perhaps he would get away with it. If Ronaldo died, there wouldn't be any witnesses to the murder. The police ought to have connected both car thefts with the murder. Maybe they'd already done so, but then it struck me that maybe they didn't *want* to understand. What did I know?

Samson Nilsen asked if it was okay to smoke. I didn't answer. He lit a cigarette and looked at me: Are you talking about that little boy?

I waited.

You like him? asked Nilsen.

The punch landed on his face. I hit out as hard as I could. As my fist hit his nose there was a nasty sound. The cigarette flew out of his mouth as his head snapped backwards. He went down, hitting his head on the wall.

The blood flooded down across his white dress shirt. My right hand was aching. The rifle in my left felt cool. Around me no one moved.

I stood there thinking that now I was finished here. I was the one who had fallen, not Samson Nilsen. I was the one who was out for the count in front of his home crowd.

I don't know what to do with you, I said to

him. I've no fucking idea what to do with people like you.

I walked down the stairs. The guests followed me with their eyes. They parted to let me through. Outside it was beginning to get light. There was a glow above the mountains, as though the sky were covered in a light mist. I heard birdsong, and the rushing of the Opo.

Down at the floating jetty I tossed the rifle into the river. It disappeared with a gentle bloop. I looked for the mother duck but couldn't see her. Just a few gulls that took off from the jetty and flew over the water. One of the biggest had a green Co-op Megastore plastic bag in its beak. It lost the bag and several other gulls squabbled over the contents that spread out across the fjord.

Back home at Tokheim I let myself in and checked the answering machine. From the floor above I heard sounds of breaking, dragging, beating. A chair was overturned, something was thrown against a wall. Ask was running amok up there. I should have done something, I should have gone up to them, but I stayed smoking by the window until the noises stopped. I waited for the police to drive up the hill and arrest me. They didn't come.

Finally I went to bed. I dreamt that our PV

had turned over and landed on its roof. There was blood and glass everywhere. My father lay in the middle of the road with a sheet covering him. Cars passed by in a steady stream and made it impossible for me to reach him. I felt the wind pressure from the cars and saw his shoes sticking out from beneath the white sheet. His left hand was visible too. He was still holding on to the steering wheel.

44

It was raining when I woke up. At last. Drops fell on my forehead and on my chest. I sat up in bed and realised the duvet was damp. The rain was coming from the ceiling. The drops were falling from the ceiling down into the room.

I dressed and went upstairs. No one answered when I rang. I pushed open the door and called out. No one answered. I called out again as I went into the living room. I didn't want to get mown down by Ask. He was quite capable of it.

The floor was covered with water. Newspapers and clothes floated around along with the remains of a pizza, bottles, paperback books. The desk had been overturned and the drawers emptied. In the bathroom all the taps were on. I turned them off and went back into the living room.

I stood there staring at the photographs that lay strewn across the floor. Hundreds of portrait photos. Blondes. Brunettes. Black girls. Thai girls. All smiling, all trying to pose professionally. Some pictures had been taken in photo booths, others in studios. Some were showing too much tit, too much thigh, others were prim and proper and serious.

I picked up one photo of a heavily made-up young woman. I imagined her sitting in front of the mirror on the day she was going to have her picture taken, how she wanted to make herself look pretty. On the back of the photograph were a few handwritten lines in English: *I know that you exist. Light from a window. Like a little star.*

From somewhere down the hall I heard coughing and waded into the bedroom. Ask sat smoking on the bed. He looked up at me as I entered, but it was as though he were somewhere far away and none of this was real.

What happened? I asked.

Ask didn't answer. I thought he must have killed Mumuki. He'd killed her, and she was lying dead somewhere in the apartment.

Is she dead? I asked.

Yes, she's dead.

Where is she?

I don't know. She just died.

What do you mean?

She died. She left me.

Is she dead, or has she left you?

She's dead. She left me.

Where is she?

She packed last night and went into Odda.

So she's not dead?

She's left me.

I breathed a little easier. I thought they must have had a fight and she'd left him. He'd gone crazy, so she'd packed her things and left. I was glad. I hoped she would never come back. I walked towards the living room, but Ask called after me.

Are you leaving too? he asked.

You got a better idea?

I want her to come back, said Ask.

A bit late for that now, I said.

I don't know what to do to get her back again, he said.

Get yourself a black one, I said.

You know, said Ask. I thought I would be the one to leave her. I thought she was something I could manage without.

I didn't answer. The guy would have to sort it out himself. I couldn't help him. All the same, there was something about him that made me feel sorry for him. I saw the big fist scraping through the hair, the thick fingers that stubbed out the cigarette.

I went out into the living room again. I rang the fire service and the insurance company. The TV was on. Four couples were competing to win a dream wedding in Las Vegas. They had to find a ring in a wedding cake. I'd been up here after Ask and Mumuki's wedding. I couldn't really understand why they'd invited me, but then they had to invite someone. Things had been very quiet in the room until they'd had enough to drink.

Down in my apartment I packed a suitcase and got into the car. Only now did I notice the heat of the sun. I considered driving up to Hjøllo to my parents, but couldn't bear the thought of it. If they hadn't written about Irene in the papers yet they would do soon enough. As soon as Irene was officially declared missing they'd start. I wound down the window and lit a cigarette. I saw the house disappear in the wing mirror. It was a house with rain inside.

I turned on the local radio as I drove in towards Odda. The mayor was being interviewed live. They were going to open a new skate park in Eide. He said a fantastic number of positive things were happening in Odda right now. I drove past Chinatown and caught a glimpse of Mumuki outside. She was wearing a red kimono. She smiled.

I called in at the office to check my e-mails and read the net news. There was nothing about Irene. The Serbs had been released. No reason was given, nor whether there were other suspects. It meant no one would be talking. If the Serbs had been accused, then they at least would have started talking.

At the Hardanger Hotel the receptionist tutted when I asked for a room.

Are you leaving home, Robert? she asked.

Summer can't be trusted, I replied.

She laughed and said I would be in Room 409.

I picked up the tabloids from the newsstand and took the lift to the fourth floor. The room smelt of dust. The wall-paper looked faded, and the walls were hung with pictures of Odda in the old days. I drew the curtains and tossed the papers on to the bedside table without reading them. I sat down on the bed in the half-light. At regular intervals the lift went up and down. Otherwise all was quiet.

It's always quiet when you're going down. Usually people pretend to be your friend. They ring you when you're on your way up or when they can get something out of you. Now I was living at the same hotel as the journalists. Perhaps I even had some of them as my neighbours. But today none of them had called. When you sink, all is silence.

It struck me that there is something dream-like about people at a hotel. Hotel guests have no roots and no goals, only a beginning and an end. They drink a beer at the bar. They laugh. They call home. They argue. They make love. They sit alone on the edge of the bed.

45

I'd slept with my mobile in my shirt pocket. It vibrated. I answered. Folkedal from the hostel said he'd been told the boy had died early that morning. The police were investigating the death but at the moment had no reason to believe the death was anything other than accidental. Several eye-witnesses had seen the boy fall into the fjord.

He couldn't swim, I said.

From somewhere far away I heard Folkedal say he wanted to talk to me about what had happened but for the time being was too upset.

Didn't you say you would look after the boy? asked Folkedal.

I couldn't answer. I just felt myself sinking down through the room, the way a coin sinks through water and comes to rest at the bottom.

Didn't you say I could count on you? asked Folkedal.

I hung up and lay on the bed. I dug out the bottle I'd packed in my suitcase. I thought I wanted to disconnect, turn off, be gone. I drank. I was so parched I couldn't get enough. I drank until the hotel bed began to sail.

I sat up and stared at the wall to make the room stop. It was my fault. I was the one who'd killed him. I thought of his hair, the sort of hair that makes you want to touch it and stroke it. I saw him the way he was, lying on the hospital bed. He was so fine, so fine.

I slept and dreamt that I shaved off all my skin. I was sitting in a chair in an empty room. I got up and peeled the wallpaper off the walls. A different wallpaper with a different pattern appeared. I peeled that one off, but always a new wallpaper appeared.

I woke up again. I didn't know where I was. I slept and dreamt that I was the one lying under the sheet in the middle of the road. I was the one holding the steering wheel in my left hand. Weegee stood over me and took a photograph. I was dead, yet I could see the expressions on the faces of the curious onlookers crowding behind the police cordon. Weegee with his hat on his head and his cigar in his mouth grinned broadly. His flash flared.

I felt a cool breeze on my forehead. Sunlight reflected down from the ceiling. Mumuki sat on the edge of the bed and stroked my cheek. She said she was sorry for what had happened. She asked what she could do to make things right. I said she shouldn't worry about it. She said that I'd saved her. I was exultant. I had saved someone. I'd done a good deed. I was a noble person. Mumuki danced in the room.

Don't you just love hotel rooms? she asked.

I laughed.

Don't you love waking up in a hotel room and just lying there?

I opened my eyes and saw clouds drifting through the room. It would start to rain soon. Soon the summer would be over. The river rose in the room and carried off the bedside table, the television, the pictures on the wall. I was floating in the room. I was floating in something I couldn't do anything about. I was floating in something I could do something about.

He is dead, I wanted to say out loud. He is dead, I wanted to say over and over again, to take the power out of the words. But my voice was gone. My throat was dry, and I could hardly swallow.

I thought of something Irene once said when I asked her what she liked best about me. We'd made love in her Volkswagen, as the snow layered down across Øyna and blanketed the windows. We had the heater and the radio on. She had kissed me and answered that I read Frank O'Hara to her. I was the only one who read Frank O'Hara to her.

I thought of her mouth next to mine. I thought of her arms around my arms. Her legs around my hips. The small breasts against my chest. I whispered to her. Get on top of me, I whispered. Cover me. Make me disappear.

I slept again and dreamt that Ronaldo had been arrested. He'd tried to steal gum from a vending machine but got his thumb caught in it. I sat holding him as he shook his thumb in the air to ease the pain. A policeman tried to pull Ronaldo away from me. I held on. I wrapped my arms around him. I lost him. Lost him.

The phone rang. I rolled over on my side and reached out for the bedside table. I missed. By the time I'd fished the phone up from the floor the connection had been lost. I couldn't sleep. Suddenly the call seemed vital.

The hotel was silent. Light from outside was reflected on the ceiling. Some trailers drove by in the night. The phone rang again. I said hello. There was silence at the other end. All I heard was my own breathing.

Hello, said a familiar voice.

I couldn't answer.

Are you there? she asked.

Even now I couldn't answer.

Were you sleeping? she asked.

Where are you? I asked.

I'm in the phone box.

What phone box?

You know, the phone box.

I didn't know what to say. I had so many questions.

Just one thing, she said. Do you remember the first time you kissed me?

Yes.

Do you remember the first time you kissed my breast?

Yes, the right one.

No, the left. You always get that wrong.

It was the right.

The left. I can still feel it. Your lips on my left breast. That's how I know. I can still feel it, Robert.

Where are you? I asked.

She was silent.

I feel you pulling down my bra, she said next. I feel you bending your head and kissing my breast. I stroke your hair as you're kissing my breast. I feel it all over my body. You're kissing my left breast.

Where are you, my love?

She didn't answer.

Tell me where you are, my love?

That's what I wanted to tell you, she said. I just wanted you to know that.

Where are you?

She said goodnight and hung up.

I climbed off the bed and dressed quickly. I took the lift down and hurried through the empty Reception. Outside it was raining. The rain made the night dark. I ran to the telephone box by the bus terminal. That was the box she used to ring me from. One of the old-fashioned types. Light fell on the phone. The air seemed used, as though the molecules of some previous conversation still hung there.

I got the car and drove to the house up at Erraflot. An outside light burnt by the entrance. Otherwise everything was in darkness. I drove on. No one about. The only sign of life was the light from the headlamps that dissolved in the rain and was swallowed up by the black asphalt.

46

The chimes from the ice-cream van woke me. The melody was the same as the one they used for *Down Your Way* on TV. It was a little after two. I got up and opened the curtains. Odda lay out there fully exposed, as though the place had been blitzed. Kids swarmed around the ice-cream van. I guessed it was Saturday, since there were so many people out in the square.

I lay down on the bed again. It was as though my whole life was running away through my fingers, and this was no longer my town. I heard laughter from the next room. Then a bang. More laughter. I didn't know what to do. I longed to be a part of something bigger. For someone to look after me and take decisions for me. Frank should have shot me. Someone should have shot me.

I picked up the newspapers from the bedside table. The thought of reading them had been unbearable. All of them had written about the murder, but none had mentioned that Irene was missing. *VG* had a feature about Pedersen where he said how much his son used to love driving the ice-cream van.

Ronaldo was covered in a tiny paragraph. A nine-year-old boy. No name. No identity. I wondered what Ronaldo had thought when he fell into the fjord. What his last thought had been. Had he thought of me? Did he think of his father landing in the seaplane to rescue him?

My mother called on the mobile. She asked if I'd been told. I said I hadn't been told.

Haven't you spoken to Frank? she asked.

No, I answered.

I knew it all the time, said my mother. Everything will be all right in the end, Robert.

What did you know?

My mother said that Irene had called earlier in the day. She was back in Odda. She had said that she had needed to be alone for a while. She just wanted to be completely alone for a few days.

That's the way it is sometimes, said my mother.

I guess so, I said.

Don't you think the idea has occurred to me too, to have a few days entirely alone?

What did Frank say?

He's just happy she's home again. You know, your brother's a gentleman.

Oh yeah?

She waited. Then she said: Aren't you two friends any more?

Oh yes.

Aren't you happy, Robert?

Yes, I'm happy.

You don't sound all that happy.

I'm very happy she's come back.

My mother said it was such a lovely day. The sun was shining, summer was here, and Irene was back. She'd even managed to track Father down. He'd disappeared early in the morning when he went out to buy the papers. Fortunately they'd called from the Cinderella Tavern. He was there now.

Did he walk all the way out there? I asked.

Yes. I spoke to him on the phone; he wants you to go and pick him up.

Why?

All he said was that he wants you to fetch him.

Okay, Mother.

And then we'll have a party in the garden. We must celebrate.

I ended the call and got dressed. I could get neither the trousers nor the shirt to fit properly, even though they were my own clothes. Even my arms and legs didn't seem to work the way they usually did.

Over in the newsagent's I looked through the papers. There was nothing about Irene. There didn't seem to be anything new about the murder either. I drove out along the west side. South Fjord was like glass. The Folgefonna glacier lay like a virgin. On the hillsides farms were bursting with chlorophyll. Soon they would be selling cherries and strawberries. It was the landscape of tourist dreams.

I wondered what had happened to Irene. Why had she disappeared? Why had she come back? I would probably never get a satisfactory answer. At least other than that, even in a place like this, now and then so much crap gets stirred up that it becomes impossible to sort things out.

Out by Måge I had to brake hard. A dead dog lay in the middle of the road. A bare-chested old man was prodding it with a stick. The scene almost made me throw up. I drove round the dog and sped off.

The Cinderella Tavern was just before you get to the centre of Nå. It looked for all the world like an outsize holiday chalet with a licence to sell alcohol. I parked outside and saw my father before he saw me. He was sitting outside with a beer and a pile of newspapers in front of him. He was wearing a pair of Elvis-type sunglasses that didn't suit him. Patches of sweat showed on his pale shirt.

I sat down and got out my cigarettes.

So you've walked all the way? I asked.

I was thirsty, he said.

We sat there, staring at the South Fjord. A few sunbronzed boys were fishing down by the jetty. Cars hissed along the road. Tourists hurrying to and from their holidays. Behind us the buzz of conversation from other customers. They were watching a roundup of World Cup highlights so far. The goals were accompanied by ecstatic music. I watched Ronaldo slip past three defenders and slot the ball into the back of the net.

Shall we go home? I asked.

My father stood up at once. From his gait I could see that he was getting older. I thought that it looked as though the power had gone out of him, as though he'd set off on a long-distance run he should never have started on.

In the car he adjusted the seat and inhaled the crappy smell before winding down the window. On the way into Odda he stared straight ahead. I thought he was waiting for the right time to speak.

I said nothing.

Did you find the hole in the fence? my father asked.

No, I answered.

Again there was a silence.

I forgot to bring the newspapers from the Cinderella, my father said.

Hadn't you read them? I asked.

He didn't answer. I waited.

There was something about a Mexican, he said. He sneaked back over the border from the USA into Mexico. He was so disappointed by the USA that all he wanted to do was get back home again.

And?

And they shot the guy. As soon as he got home, they shot him.

Who's they?

The neighbours.

Why did they do that?

They thought he must be stinking rich.

But he wasn't?

He was as poor as the day he left.

As we emerged from the Eitrheim tunnel I turned on the local radio station. There was some interference before I got it tuned right. The announcer said that the Fjord Shopping Centre were having a Crazy Price sale and that there would be radio bingo later on in the evening. I thought how this town resembled a toy. Odda was a plastic toy that was almost coming apart, a toy with parts that were made to break.

We drove over the Hjøllo bridge. The Opo was higher than I could ever remember. My father said they'd rescued Dean Martini from the river bank late last night. Despite

Martini's protests the police had taken him away.

Irene's Volkswagen stood on the grass outside the house. I parked alongside. Without saying anything my father climbed out and disappeared up the steps into the garden. I went into the house. A radio was playing in the living room. Out in the kitchen my mother was singing. From the balcony door I saw the kids jumping through the water sprinkler. My brother was standing on the lawn. He was wearing his aviator shades, shorts and an unbuttoned shirt. He was getting really fat.

I went out on to the balcony. Irene came up the steps from the garden. She was barefoot and wearing her white summer frock. She stopped in front of me, took off her sunglasses and smiled. I met her gaze and waited, without speaking. We stood like that for a while. The heat closed in around me. My head was working slowly.

I'd better help your mother in the kitchen, she said, and slipped past me.

I caught the scent of her perfume as she went by. Nothing else. Only the faintest trace of perfume. I stood there in the sun. I thought that she had smiled the same way on that New Year's Eve when both Frank and I had asked her to dance. Sorry, I chose him.

In the shade of the apple tree my mother had laid the table. White plates on a blue-checked tablecloth. It was laid for seven. I had a vision of the days to come. The Saturday evenings. The Sunday mornings. The weeks. The months. The dinners. The talk. The laughter. The sun that would shine. The rain that would come.

My brother had noticed me. He stared as he sprayed the kids with the garden hose. The kids shrieked and called to me.

Are you joining in, Uncle Robert? they shouted.

I waved.

Come and join in, Uncle Robert!

I turned and went inside again. The air in the room was drowsy and still. I heard a voice on the radio saying it looked like being a record summer. From the kitchen came the sound of meat sizzling in fat. My mother hummed. Through the open door I saw Irene with her back to me.

I went out to the car and got in.

Other titles published by
The House of Ulverscroft:

THE MAN WHO COULDN'T LOSE

Roger Silverwood

Detective Inspector Michael Angel and his team investigate another puzzling and chilling case of murder in the south Yorkshire town of Bromersley. Wheelchair-bound millionaire businessman, Joshua Gumme, has the Midas touch. He's successful with women and in business, and at card games he always wins. But whilst everybody knows he cheats, they just don't know how. So it is no surprise to find his body floating in the River Don. At the same time, Angel's investigations lead him on the track of two dangerous crooks. He attempts to find and arrest them — but they've got plans for him.

THE CORPORAL WORKS OF MURDER

Sister Carol Anne O'Marie

Sister Mary Helen is once more in the middle of a murder case. She holds a dying young woman, shot in the street outside the Refuge for homeless women. Grieving over the loss of life, Mary Helen spots something strange about the victim. Her ragged clothing is at odds with her healthy looking unblemished skin; her perfect teeth are white and unstained. Her appearance belies that of a woman living in poverty on the streets. With the weapons of her logical mind, will Sister Mary Helen solve the case and prove once again to be the bane of Inspector Gallagher's life?

THE FATE OF WOMEN

Lawrence Williams

Every police officer has a case that will haunt him. For Detective Sergeant Jack Bull it is the case known as the Fate of Women. Someone has developed a solution to the problem of responding to violence against women. That person is murdering rapists discharged from prison after serving derisory short sentences. For Detective Sergeant Jack Bull, the stress is partially caused by his ambivalence towards wanting the serial murderer caught. But greater worry comes from the possibility that he too will be murdered . . . Jack is pushed to his limits as the investigation leads to its tragic conclusion.

HOW TO SUCCEED IN MURDER

Margaret Dumas

Newlywed Charley Fairfax's intention of living happily ever after with her husband is undermined when Jack is hired to investigate a suspicious death at a San Francisco software company. Apparently, high-tech has some low-life elements. To help Jack, Charley needs to get a job. Work experience for Charley and her fellow members of the repertory theatre may have been gained from a production of *How to Succeed in Business Without Really Trying* — but that doesn't stop them going undercover to find a killer. And if only people would stop trying to murder them, Charley and Jack might get to take their honeymoon . . .